Misadventures of a Cryptid Hunter

D1522024

Discover other titles by Michael Kelso

This book is an original work of fiction. Names, characters, places, and incidents either are the product of the author's imagination or are used fictitiously. Any resemblance to actual persons, living, dead, events, and/or locations is entirely coincidental.

As always, you can't have horror stories of deadly creatures without some violence. This book is no exception. There are scenes of violence, blood, adult language, and adult themes. Reader discretion is advised.

This book would not be possible without the support of many people.

First of all, my family, who have been very supportive of my writing.

My cover designer, https://www.fiverr.com/kingof_designer?source=gig_page

Youtube Creepypasta narrator, Mr Creeps https://www.youtube.com/@MrCreeps

My amazing Beta readers, Emily Haynes, Sandy Beebe, Sherri McCune, and last but certainly not least, Boris Bacic. As always, his help and advice remain invaluable. Please support his works as well. https://linktr.ee/Author.Boris.Bacic

From the author.

This book is a little different from my other horror books. It started out as another short story, but the main character was so fun to write, I just had to keep going and see how it turned out.

You'll find the chapters are considerably longer than I usually write. This is because every chapter was written as its own short story within the larger overall story. It includes a good amount of humor that I hope everyone enjoys. The main character's snarky attitude helps move things along as he deals with untold horrors that would make the rest of us (including me) run away screaming.

The story wasn't meant to be one hundred percent accurate. Creative liberties were taken for entertainment value. If you're reading through and focusing on how a certain cryptid wouldn't act the way it did in the book, you've missed the point.

This book was written to scare the reader as well as make them laugh.

So sit back, strap in, and prepare for a page turning, chill inducing, laugh out loud adventure.

I hope you have as much fun reading it as I did writing it.

Chapter 1

I hate being a park ranger. There, I said it. It's nice to finally get it off my chest. It's not like there's any one specific thing that makes it so bad, it's a combination. The pay sucks, the health insurance is non-existent, dear God don't ever forget to hose yourself down with bug spray during the warmer months. I have a case of it I keep in my car. I found out the hard way when I was down near the lake and was set upon by a swarm of mosquitos. And the ticks get into places you wouldn't imagine. These are the minor annoyances.

There's also the other part of the job, the dangerous part. I'm not talking about people being idiots and having to swoop down from the top of a ravine to rescue them. Yeah, that's there. In my opinion that's called natural selection. If they were close enough to the edge to fall, then that's on them. No, I'm not talking about those incidents either, I'm talking about real danger.

I'm not supposed to say anything, but I'm tired of the code of silence. That's why I'm writing this. It goes without saying that I won't use anyone's real name, including the park. That should keep me out of trouble.

I started working here as park ranger around a year ago. It seemed nice at first to get out and enjoy nature. I'm sure nature would laugh at that since she seems to be set on killing people. Between storms, falling trees, landslides, wildfires, and not to mention cryptids, nature is not exactly man's best friend, at least in this park.

Every evening at dusk some of us rangers drive around to the trailheads to make sure there's no cars sitting around. If there is, we take the license number and call the police to see if the person has been reported missing. If there are no cars, we lock the gates.

This evening I had just finished locking the gate down by the lake. It had been a while since I'd been near any restrooms and the nearest one was a half mile away. I was responsible for this side of the lake so I knew no other rangers would be around. I glanced left and right, then whipped out and added a little more fluid to the lake.

As I was relieving myself, this huge, hairy creature stepped out of the forest around fifty feet away from me and approached the lake. It bent over pulling water out of the lake with its massive hands and bringing it up to its mouth to drink. After the third handful, it noticed me for the first time. It saw what I was doing, then spat the mouthful of water back into the lake.

We both froze.

You know that 'Oh crap' moment when you catch someone doing something they shouldn't at the same time you're doing something you shouldn't? Like when you're on duty and coming out of the liquor store with a brown bag and you see a coworker buying a bag of weed? You both stare at each other hoping that the other one will be the one to feel guilty and walk away first, but neither of you do, you just stand there.

That's what we did. We just stood there looking at each other this creature and I.

Was I scared? Hell, yeah I was scared. This thing was freakin huge. You remember that part in Star Wars where Han tells Threepio that Wookies are known to rip people's arms out of their sockets. That's what I was thinking this thing might do. I mean it was big enough to give Chewie a swirlie.

The thought of my arms being forcefully and painfully removed from my body bounced around in my head so much I started sweating. They say animals can smell fear. I bet I smelled like I had just walked out of a 'Saw' movie marathon.

Neither one of us moved. Me out of total terror, him out of… how the hell should I know what that thing was thinking? All I knew was it wasn't running away. I didn't take that as a good sign. I took that as him looking at me and someone in the background ringing the dinner bell. Finally, after a long moment of this insane standoff, my shaking hand reached for my phone.

Much to my surprise and relief, it took off into the woods at inhuman speed.

Against my better judgement, I followed as best I could but soon lost sight of it. I came back to the shoreline and found huge footprints. I took pictures with my phone and went to the station to show everyone.

"That's super," Ron said with a laugh. "Did you get a picture of the tooth fairy too?"

The room erupted with laughter as all the rangers, even the ones I considered to be friends, turned on me.

"No that would be a Fae," said Sharon. "Not a sasquatch. Don't you know anything, Ron?"

"Did it give you any beef jerky?" Jeff said causing the group to erupt with even more laughter.

"Now come on," Nancy said. "Let's be realistic."

My hopes soared that someone might believe me.

"You don't really think there's any beef in that jerky do you?" Nancy said.

My hopes crashed like the Obama economy.

"Hey, shut up all you idiots," Dell said pulling me aside. "Let me see that phone."

I handed it to him feeling my hopes rise again.

He looked through the pictures one by one. His face was set. I couldn't' read his emotions. He didn't seem to react with surprise or disbelief. When he was done looking through them he scrolled back and deleted every picture that had anything to do with the creature.

"What the hell?" I said, grabbing my phone.

"I'm doing you a favor," he said. "You don't wanna go down that road. It only leads to bad things."

I stared at my phone in shock. I couldn't believe someone I trusted, someone I looked up to, the most senior ranger in the station had just destroyed evidence of this mythical creature's existence.

"But it was real," I said. "I saw it."

Chuckles sounded from around the room. Dell turned and silenced them with a look.

"Why don't you take tomorrow off and get your head clear?" he said.

I found myself nodding and not really sure why as he guided me out of the station toward my car.

"Enjoy yourself," he said. "Go do something relaxing. You've had a hard day."

I started toward my car, Dell watching me the entire time. As soon as he stepped back inside, I could hear another roar of laughter. I knew it was at my expense.

I got into my car in a daze. It wasn't until I stared at my phone that I realized just how violated I felt.

I drove home and sat in the kitchen staring at the wall. 'I know I saw it.' I kept telling myself. I pondered what to do with no evidence and no one to back me up. An idea came to me. I started looking for bigfoot traps online. I looked up how to trap a bigfoot and got some very interesting ideas. The next day I went and bought some bear traps.

When I drove to work the following morning, I got there early and quietly transferred my bear traps to the state truck I would be using that day.

I went inside and greeted the other rangers. They all seemed aloof and holding back like they were waiting for something to happen.

I rounded the corner to the lockers and found out what. My locker had been covered in bigfoot pictures. There was even one with a picture of a naked woman and Chewbacca's head taped over hers. The caption written in said, "Come find me, big boy."

This is why I hate people.

I did my best to ignore it as the titters and chuckles sounded behind me.

I said nothing and went to my truck. I sat there for a long time trying to get the rage to bleed off, but all I could think of was revenge.

That taught me the hard lesson, 'Keep your mouth shut.' I learned that lesson well, but the damage was already done. The other rangers were already calling me a freak and a joke.

That pissed me off but also strengthened my resolve. It would've been easy to quit right there but I was determined to prove myself. That I was as good as they were. That I wasn't crazy. That this thing really existed.

As the man said, two outta three ain't bad.

I started patrolling down by the lake more often, looking for my prey where I had seen it last. But I had the sinking suspicion that it was watching me. That it knew I was hunting it. I tried to be nonchalant about it at first. I'd just drive by, looking around like a good ranger should. But after a while, I started getting impatient. I would spend more time there than the rest of my route. It got to the point where people would come up to me and ask for help, but I would ignore them or shuttle them off to another ranger.

I started getting proactive in my hunt. I found a deer carcass near the place I'd seen the creature and set the bear traps up around it.

Then I staked out the area and waited.

For a long time.

People came up to me, I ignored them. Animals came up to me,

I ignored them. The only thing I was focused on was finding my prey.

Morning turned to afternoon turned to evening with no results. I sighed in resignation when it came time to close the gates. I decided to go home and let the traps do the work for me.

The next morning, I overslept. I drove like a madman to get to work. More specifically to get back to my stakeout. Imagine my surprise when I came back and found I had caught something in my trap... a fellow ranger.

Ron lay on the ground screaming. I went over to help him.

"Are you ok?" I said.

"No, dumbass, I have a giant metal jaw attached to my leg."

I fumbled with the trap trying to get it open only to have it snap shut on his leg again.

"What the hell are you doing?" he said. "Are you too stupid to open a trap?"

I stopped and stared at him. "At least I'm not stupid enough to step into one."

"Screw you!"

I stood to leave.

"Where are you going?"

I whipped around on him.

"Screw you," I said. "I come over here to help you and you're treating me like some piece of crap. Get out of your own damn trap."

I started walking away.

"Ok," he said.

I stopped and turned.

"Ok, what?"

"Ok, I'm sorry. Will you please help me out of this trap?"

I paused for a moment then went back.

"Alright, I've never opened a trap before," I lied. "Tell me what to do."

"These are the springs," he said. "Press down on them and It'll open the jaws."

Once the jaws were open, he pulled his injured leg free.

"Thank God," he said checking out his injured leg. "Who put that trap there anyway."

"No clue," I lied.

I drove Ron straight to the hospital to get him taken care of. Once he was in a room and being treated, I left.

But there was the matter of the illegal bear trap that had injured a park ranger. Dell was not happy. He pulled me into his office.

"I can't believe this happened," he said. "I've known Ron for years. He's a good friend and a good ranger. The person responsible for this will pay. I'll see him strung up by his entrails."

"Yes, sir," I said.

"This should never happen on park grounds. It's a deliberate assault and I won't rest until I see Ron's killer behind bars."

"He's not dead, sir."

"Whatever, you get the point," he said. "And what do you know about this?"

"Me," I said feigning ignorance. "Why would you ask me?"

He shot me a steely glare.

"You know exactly why," he said.

I was feeling the metaphorical handcuffs click closed around my wrists.

"Because you didn't listen to me and let this bigfoot thing go," he said. "Other rangers have seen you hanging around where you saw that thing. I'm thinking maybe you saw the person who set that trap."

I took a breath, feeling the cuffs fall off my wrists.

"There have been a few unsavory types hanging around," I said.

"I want you to track them down and find out who did this to one of my rangers," he said slamming his fist on his desk.

"Yes, sir," I said as I walked out of his office.

I couldn't believe it. I was off the hook. I was in charge of my own investigation. Stopping to think about it, it made perfect sense that he chose me. It was a crap job that no one else wanted to do. But I was going to do it to the absolute best of my ability, I thought sarcastically. 'Yes, sir, I won't rest until I'm brought to justice. You can count on me, sir.'

I waited until I was a mile down the road before I started laughing.

I went to the crime scene and explored it very carefully. Back and forth, over and over I went through the area until there were no tracks anywhere that weren't mine. Of course, the only tracks before were mine too, and of course, Ron's.

As an added bonus to tracking myself, I was able to do it in the area of the sighting continuing my search for the creature. It was win-win for me.

'Thank you, Ron, you idiot, for blundering into that trap and giving me the best assignment I could possibly have.' I thought.

As the days went by and I searched for myself in vain, I came across an area not too far from the lake where there was a cave with a well-worn path to it. At first, I thought it was a bear cave, but then I found a couple of the tracks that had been deleted off my phone by a certain ranger.

I took pictures of the tracks and made sure I sent them to myself by email. I also kept my mouth shut about it. At least to all my idiot coworkers. My mind playfully wondered how many more I could trick into a bear trap or maybe something worse.

I smiled as I chided myself for such thoughts.

Suddenly I felt something was wrong. The birds stopped singing. I turned to find the creature standing four feet from me. I was amazed at how silent it moved. My amazement quickly gave way to fear as a yellow river ran down the inside of my pants.

It was even more huge up close. At least eight feet tall and completely covered in brown hair. It had bared its teeth and was flexing its massive hands.

For some reason I don't think it liked me very much. Go figure.

It lunged at me with impossible speed.

I tried to dodge but my boot got stuck on a tree root and I tripped. I fell backwards and landed hard on my back, knocking the wind out of me.

I lay there, helpless, at the mercy of this beast. All it had to do was carry me into its cave and I would never be seen again. Except for in smelly little piles hours later. That was a happy thought.

I tried to regain my normal breathing, surprised that it hadn't dragged me away yet.

As I came around and the stars floating around my head turned back into trees, I saw the creature lying face down a few yards from me.

I rose slowly and approached it. I could see its back rising and falling, so I knew it was still breathing. I took out my phone and took pictures just in case it didn't kill me or in case it got up and ran away. I even leaned close and took a selfie with it in the background.

Just then it took a slightly deeper breath and I skittered away. When it didn't jump up and rip my arms out of my sockets, I took a closer look. There was a little blood lying beside its head which was resting on top of a big rock. Apparently when it lunged at me it wasn't counting on me falling and it dove right into a rock. Knocked itself cold.

This was it. The golden goose had pulled a muscle in its wing while it flew over me and landed in my lap.

I ran to the truck, grabbed the tranquilizer gun and a lot of netting. As I ran back the thought of it not being there drove me to distraction. All my hard work of lucking into this perfect scenario would've been for nothing. I ran as fast as I could carrying a big net on my back and prayed it was still there.

When I got there it was stirring and trying to get up. I dropped the net and fumbled with the tranquilizer gun, nearly shooting myself in the process until I finally aimed. It saw me just as I pointed the gun at it. Our eyes locked. It was a magical moment until I squeezed the trigger and sent him back to lala land.

He probably wasn't going to be too happy when he woke though. I accidentally shot him in the crotch.

I made sure to reload the gun just in case, then tried to roll him over onto the netting. He felt like he weighed a thousand pounds.

I racked my brain on how to get him out of there and eventually came up with a solution. I backed the truck up through a half mile of trees, leaving scratches on the sides and almost leaving a rearview mirror behind. I managed to get close enough to hook the net onto the trailer hitch. I dragged him out to the road and stopped to figure out my next move.

My house was ten miles away. If I dragged him the whole way there all I would have left would be Bigfoot burger. I couldn't lift him and it was after hours so there was no one else around to help me get him into the truck bed. Not that I really wanted anyone else to see him.

I panned around and found the solution. There was a small embankment maybe four feet high. I drove the truck onto it and then drove very carefully straight down it. I was terrified I would flip the truck end over end and that would end my little adventure. But I just kept moving slowly as the front wheels touched down and kept going. Next was the tricky part. I got the back wheels on the ground then gunned it forward and slammed it in reverse.

His head was hanging over the edge when I backed up and I accidentally pinned it between the truck gate and the dirt bank. I pulled forward a little and grabbed the netting, pulling with every ounce of strength I had. Ever so slowly his prone body inched forward until he reached the tipping point and rolled into the bed of the truck. When he flopped down one of his feet hit the back window and shattered it.

'Great,' I thought. 'Hey boss, when I was capturing the creature you said doesn't exist in the company vehicle I broke a window. Is that covered by our insurance?'

I was breathing hard until I was done. I covered him with a tarp and drove away, wracking my brain about where I would take him. As I was thinking I passed a storage unit that was somewhat remote. It was just off the backroad I was on and it didn't seem like much traffic passed this way.

I called up and rented a unit with my credit card then showed up and backed the truck up to it.

My cargo was starting to stir again as I arrived so I gave it another dose of tranquilizer and dragged it off the truck as best I could. Meaning it flopped over and nearly crushed me, then not all of it was inside and I couldn't close the door, so I turned the truck around and gently pushed it inside with the front bumper before closing and locking the door.

Next came the tricky part. I couldn't go on Craigslist and advertise, 'One Bigfoot, slightly used, fifty million OBO.' Fortunately, I knew a guy who had a cousin's brother who knew another guy's best friend who knew someone who knew someone else who might be able to get me in contact with someone who doesn't exist.

I printed a few of the pictures, wrote a number with a lot of zeros in it and sent it through the information chain.

I got a phone call two hours later from someone who doesn't exist. He met me at the storage unit with a lot of heavily armed men dressed in black combat gear and no identifying patches.

When we got there the door was under assault. It had lots of newly formed dents in it and the sides were looking like they weren't going to hold much longer. My 'friend' apparently had woken up and wasn't very happy with his new surroundings. I offered to open the door just an inch and hit him with another tranq dart, but the man waved me off.

The heavily armed gentlemen worked with practiced precision. They flung open the door and threw a containment net over him as he tried to run past them. Within moments he was incapacitated.

As they carried him out his eyes landed on me. They narrowed and he let out a menacing growl.

"I'd say you've made a new friend," The Man said, handing me a business card with a number on it and nothing else.

"What's this for?" I said.

"If you come across any more creatures of such a mythical nature, give me a call. Maybe we can help with the capture of the next one."

"Are you nuts? You saw that thing. It's huge and it wants to kill me."

"And yet here you are, very much alive," he reached into his pocket and pulled out a check. "And very wealthy."

I peered at the check and then back at him.

He grinned. "Might I suggest you not spend too much and raise suspicions?"

"So, you would pay me this much for each one of these things I found?"

He nodded.

"And you would help me catch it?"

He nodded again.

"Looks like you just bought yourself a park ranger," I said offering my hand.

He shook it.

"Pleasure doing business with you," he said then turned and walked away.

***

Temptation is a terrible thing. I was tempted to buy a brand-new Ferrari and drive it to work just to shove it in the noses of the idiots who made fun of me. But then I realized that success is the best revenge. If I could nab another creature or two, I could buy my own little island and retire. I'm thinking maybe Hawaii.

My 'investigation' into the bear trap took me to a place where I've heard there's been some trouble lately with missing hikers. Not that I really care about the hikers. In this park I think we should rename the trails for which cryptid hunts on it. That way when these hikers ignore the warnings and blunder into the dens of these dangerous creatures, they'll only have themselves to blame.

I'm thinking maybe I can make my job easier by buying the land that has the cryptid I'm looking for and then clearcut all the trees so it has no place to hide. I know what you're thinking, it would just run away to another spot. Not the way I would clear-cut. Start with a hundred machines on the outside of the property and work our way in to the center so it has nowhere to go.

As I scanned around the land and daydreamed a hiker came running up to me.

"Please, you need to help me," she said.

"What's the problem?" I said feeling less than interested.

"My husband and brother, they were attacked."

"By an animal?"

She lowered her eyes.

"I don't really know what it was. It seemed… unnatural."

My ears perked up and I became laser-focused on helping this poor woman.

"Don't worry, Ma'am. Show me where it happened and I'll take care of it."

"Thank God," she said as we started down the trail. "I was worried you wouldn't believe me."

"Trust me, ma'am. I want to find out what happened as much as you do."

Chapter 2

You know what a love-hate relationship is, right? I think everyone has one at some point. My point was the last year or so of my life. I hated being a park ranger, but I loved the perks it came with.

Maybe I should explain that better. The perks don't come directly from the job, they come from the appearance of the job. I tell people I'm a park ranger, my boss thinks I'm a park ranger, even my idiot coworkers think I'm a park ranger, but it's just not so. That's only for appearances. I'm actually a cryptid hunter. I started calling myself that last month after successfully capturing an adult bigfoot.

What did I do with it? I sold it to a group of people who didn't have names or ranks but gave me lots of money for it. I use the park ranger persona to stay low-key and keep hunting other cryptids. Do I do it for the greater good? Hell no, don't make me laugh. I do it for the money.

I help people in the process, but it's purely unintentional. For instance, this woman came to me crying that her husband and brother were missing. When she explained that something had attacked them, something that didn't look like any animal she'd ever seen, I knew I had some money on the line. I mean, umm, I knew I had to help that poor woman find her family, yeah, that's it.

We walked down the trail, my senses on high alert looking for any signs of trouble. Birds were singing so that was a good sign that nothing was in the area. In other words, it was a bad sign for me.

We got to her campsite and the place looked like a tornado had hit it, or my place after a bender. I searched around for tracks but couldn't find any. That in itself told me something.

"Ma'am," I said to the frazzled woman who was so shell-shocked she was cleaning up the campsite. "Did you hear anything before your husband was taken?"

"Like what?"

"Like a rushing or a flapping?"

She stared at me like she was rethinking the whole 'I'm so glad you believe me' thing.

"You mean like a bird?"

"Yes, ma'am."

"I don't think so," she said picking up plastic cups and putting them in the trash.

I wanted to tell her not to disturb anything, but I figured this was her way of coping, so I let her go.

As I searched the campsite for clues I found something I'm sure the woman didn't want me to, a small pool of blood. I used that as my ground zero to search for other clues. Once she saw me paying close attention to one spot, she came over to see what had caught my attention.

She put her hand to her mouth and started breathing erratically.

"Is that,,, ?"

"Yes, ma'am, it's blood," I said waiting for her to fall into hysterics.

To my great surprise, she didn't. She merely fell to the ground and stared at the spot in shock. I took this moment to call for assistance on my radio. I gave them the coordinates and told them we had two missing hikers who were possibly the victims of an animal attack.

Dell, my boss, hesitated for a moment and then asked me what kind of animal. I told him I didn't know but couldn't find any tracks.

Just FYI, Dell didn't believe me when I told him I'd found a bigfoot. He deleted the pictures off my phone I had taken of the creature's footprints. Yeah, it's safe to say I hate my boss. But he'll get his someday.

He sent a couple of rangers out, Nancy and Jeff.

I won't say I hate them, but I will say they laughed me out of the station when I told the story about finding Bigfoot, so yeah, not my favorite people.

Nancy made a beeline for the lady hiker.

"What's your name?" she said.

"Ellyn," the woman said not even looking at Nancy.

I guess that's one of those questions I should've asked.

"Are you alright, Ellyn?" Nancy said. "Can I get you anything? Do you want me to drive you home while they look for your family?"

It all sounded good. It sounded like she was really concerned for this poor woman. I knew it was total bullshit.

"I'd rather stick around in case they show up," the woman said.

"Yes, of course," Nancy said. "But you know that might not be for a while."

"Maybe if you were out searching instead of trying to coddle me they'd be back already."

I liked this woman.

Nancy plastered her best park ranger smile on her face and stormed off into the campsite to pretend to look for clues while she fumed about the hiker who had the nerve to think she knew what was good for herself.

Jeff stepped in and took over the show, I mean the investigation. He started ordering us to go in different directions and fan out to look for the men.

I walked off in a random direction just to get away so I wouldn't be tempted to use my pepper spray on him.

The farther I got from Nancy and Jeff the better I felt. In fact, I walked so far thinking about those two idiots, (the rangers not the hikers) that I lost track of where I was going. That nearly came to a fatal end when I stumbled upon a cliff's edge with grass leading right up to it.

I stopped with my feet right at the edge of the ground, my toes were sticking out into thin air. My momentum had carried me a little too far and I was teetering over. My arms pinwheeled comically as I tried to regain my balance. It didn't help that the first thing my eyes were drawn to was the ground hundreds of feet below.

For an eternity I hung on the precipice of a horrible death as I fought against gravity. However, in reality, it was only a few seconds until I composed myself and threw my body backwards.

I lay on the ground making a mental note to buy a parachute and keep it in my backpack at all times.

The only thing worse than dying was dying rich and not having the time to spend your money.

As I sat on the ground and scanned up and down the nearly invisible edge of the cliff, I thought about building a fence along the edge. Not for the hikers, but for me.

As I contemplated how much it would cost my eyes settled on something that seemed out of place. Just visible past a row of trees, one of the large branches that jutted out of the cliff face had a nest built on it. The branch was big, probably a foot or more across and the nest was even bigger.

I pulled out my binoculars and examined it. As I did something popped its head out of the nest and glanced around. It didn't look like a bird's head. If anything, it looked more like a horse's head. I took my binoculars down and rubbed my eyes. I knew I couldn't be seeing that right.

I peered through the binoculars again and this time the creature was staring at me.

You know the expression my spine turned to ice. Well, mine turned into freakin Antarctica. The thing let out the most God-awful, piercing scream I've ever heard. It could put all those women in the horror movies to shame.

I covered my ears and closed my eyes. When the scream ended I glanced over and the thing was gone. Either that or it had ducked back into the nest.

I pulled out my phone to call The Man Who Doesn't Exist. I started dialing the number then stopped and disconnected the call. I had only turned over one cryptid to him so far. Even though he said to call if I found another, I still wasn't one hundred percent sure I had. I needed to investigate and get some pictures at least.

Against every ounce of common sense, I stood and made my way toward the nest. It wasn't easy. I could see why no one had ever reported it before. The one place where I had nearly fallen over the cliff was the one place that had enough of a clearing to even see the nest.

I was stumbling through dense forest, trying not to lose my sense of direction while still walking the tightrope between keeping the cliff in sight and falling over it.

I finally stood at the base of the tree branch that hung out over the cliff. I peeked out from behind a tree at the nest, hoping to see if the creature was there or not. Standing a mere twenty feet away from it I could see how the creature avoided being seen. The edge of the nest was five feet tall. That thing could be having a dance party in there and no one would know.

I stepped to the edge of the cliff where the branch started. Looking at it I knew there was no way I was walking out there on a tree branch that was only one foot wide. I've never wanted to walk on a high wire and I wasn't going to start today.

I turned to leave when I glanced back at the branch. On the edge of the nest was a small patch of red. I peered through my binoculars and confirmed, it appeared to be blood.

I hiked double time back to my truck, avoiding the campsite, and drove to town. I bought the most expensive drone I could find. By the time I got back to the park it was time to close the gates. I knew I wouldn't see anything tonight regardless because there wasn't enough light.

After I helped close up, I drove home and charged my new drone while reading the manual and familiarizing myself with the controls.

I woke up early and ran the drone through a few paces just to make sure I had the controls right. The camera was the most important feature I tried out and it worked like a dream.

I drove to work and went through my morning routine then volunteered to continue the search for the missing hikers. The woman had finally relented late last night and gone home.

I tried my best to remember the way to the nest but got turned around a few times before finding the cliff edge by once again nearly falling over it. I guess that's an occupational hazard of being a park ranger turned cryptid hunter.

Once I spotted the nest, I made my way there. That sounds much easier than it was when I was carrying a drone in a case the size of a large suitcase and nearly as heavy. Imagine trying to do that while navigating through heavy brush trying to stay as quiet as possible and also trying not to get lost or fall to your death.

When I cashed that first check for catching a cryptid I thought it was way too much money. Although I didn't tell them that. Now I'm starting to wonder if it was enough.

I found the opening in the trees to spot the nest, set the heavy case down and prepared the drone. I was so excited I nearly dropped the remote control.

I turned the drone on, checked the controls, and launched it straight up out of the trees. Its propellers buzzed with that distinctive drone sound as it rose majestically into the air. I nudged the control forward to hover over the nest, watching the screen the entire time. It had gone a little too high and the nest was hard to see so I began to lower it. There was something in the nest but I couldn't make it out yet.

Suddenly something rose out of the nest incredibly fast straight at the drone. My screen filled with static and I peeked out of the trees to watch my drone tumble end over end to its death on the ground far below.

I ducked back into the trees so that whatever had killed my drone didn't swing around and spot me. As I hid I checked my phone to replay the video and get some idea of what I was dealing with. When I went back through the videos and couldn't find it I realized I forgot to hit record.

I'm such an idiot sometimes.

I started sneaking out of the woods toward my truck to go get another drone. I paused and glanced back at the case I'd left behind.

'I'll let it be,' I thought. 'No use to drag it back out when I can use it as a marker for this spot. Besides, if I need to get rid of it later I'll just kick it over the cliff. What am I gonna do, arrest myself for littering?'

I made it back to my truck and went back to the store for another drone.

"Back so soon?" the cashier said. "And buying two this time. You wreck the first one already?"

"Something like that," I said pulling out a wad of cash to pay for them.

"Wow! Aren't you a park ranger?"

"Yeah."

"They must be paying a lot better than here."

"Not really."

"Then how are you affording these expensive drones?"

I realized I was blowing my cover.

"Vacation money," was the first thing that popped into my head.

"Well, have a nice vacation," he said as I walked out the door.

'Dumbass!' I thought chastising myself. 'You better think up a better excuse or stop buying stuff.'

I was so lost in my thoughts I nearly ran into my boss.

"What the hell are you doing here?"

"Umm… " was my supremely intelligent answer.

"And what the hell are those?"

My brain tried to get out in front of the situation.

"They're drones," I said. "For searching for the missing hikers."

"Really? And who authorized you to purchase those?"

"You did."

"When did I do that?"

"When you put me in charge of investigation."

"I never… "

"Remember when you put me in charge of investigating who had set the bear traps that got ranger Ron injured?"

"Yeah, but I didn't… "

"I told you some unsavory types were hanging around and you told me to track them down."

"I did say that, but… "

"How better to track them down than with an eye in the sky?"

He paused, trying to process our conversation.

"Can I get a word in now?"

"Sure."

"Who paid for this?"

"I charged it to the park service of course."

His ears grew red.

"Don't ever do that again," he said. "I don't care if I make you the head of the whole damn park service, don't ever charge anything without my consent, clear?"

"Yes, sir," I said snapping to attention.

"Get the hell outta here and go find those hikers."

"Yes, sir," I said walking away, then I paused.

"Sir?"

"What?"

"What were you doing here?"

He narrowed his eyes and growled, "None of your business."

Then he disappeared into the store.

'Dammit!' I thought. 'Why didn't I use that line?'

I headed back to the spot, drone in hand, running through my mistakes from last time when I stepped into the clearing and saw it.

The creature stood at least six feet tall. It had wings that were folded along its sides. Its head was the only thing that kept it from looking like a giant bird. The head looked like a horse.

It was sniffing at the drone case I'd left behind. I wondered why it was so interesting when I realized, 'It's picking up my scent.'

As I made my horrible realization the creature glared at me and screamed.

I'd never heard anything so brain-numbingly terrifying in my life.

I stood there, petrified as stone as the creature started toward me. It was taking those long slow steps like the T-rex in Jurassic Park. My mind finally kicked in and told me, 'Move or die, dumbass!'

I backed up and stumbled over the drone I had carried here, tumbling to the ground as the creature leapt in the air and came down with its talons out, trying to slash me open.

I rolled away as it landed on the drone case. I jumped up and ran as fast as I could into the trees. I glanced left and right, looking for better cover when I saw a patch of heavy brush. I dove into it hoping that thing wouldn't want to tear itself up chasing after me.

Thorns, jaggers, and all kinds of unyielding plants tore at my uniform until they got through to my skin. I ran until I fell then I crawled for another half mile through underbrush, creek beds, and anything else that got in my way. Eventually, I stopped because I was just exhausted.

I glanced around and saw there was no clear view of the sky and no sign of pursuit. I collapsed on my back and lay in a bed of pine needles as I caught my breath and thought about my future as a cryptid hunter or as a living human being on this planet. At the moment it seemed like the choice was one or the other.

As I stared up I saw the orange sky of sunset. I wondered if it would be the last one I saw.

The sky triggered a thought.

'It's nearly dark and I have no idea where I am, let alone where my truck is, that thing is out there somewhere, and it now knows my scent.'

I knew I had to get moving. That thing isn't the only predator in these woods. And dark is when they come out to feed.

I stood and made my way to a somewhat clear path of trees. I tried to follow beside the brush I had crawled through. Eventually, I found my way back to the clearing where my second drone sat crushed with large talon marks through the case.

I didn't even look at the nest, just snuck as quietly as possible back to my truck and drove to the station.

It was dark when I got there. I knew I would get chewed out for not helping close up for the day.

I stepped in the room and all eyes locked on me. They stared in utter shock as if I had just sprouted a second head or something.

'Do they know what I'm up to?' I thought. 'Did the kid at the store rat me out to the boss for having that wad of cash?'

"What the hell happened to you?" Sharon said approaching me.

"What do you mean?"

"You look like you went through a woodchipper."

I went to the bathroom, stared in the mirror and sure enough I was a sight. My uniform was ripped so badly it was barely hanging on me in places. There were spots and streaks of mud and blood. And my face appeared to have taken the worst of it. I had scratches all over. It seemed like the only place I wasn't scratched up was my eyes.

I stepped back into the main room to several pairs of expectant eyes. I was tempted to use the boss's earlier report and say it was none of their business, but instead, my tired brain came up with a brilliant reason that was sure to satisfy everyone.

"I fell."

I was exhausted and didn't feel like dealing with the myriad comments I could already see loading up in my coworkers' eyes, so I turned and left.

When I got home, I painfully stripped off my clothes and took a long shower.

After settling in for some supper and much-needed rest I considered my options.

Calling the man who doesn't exist seemed almost premature at this point. Yes, I had seen a cryptid face to ugly face, but what if it decided the nest was getting too much traffic?

I didn't want to go out to that nest again. And I wasn't sure if I could force myself to do it.

I thought back to my first encounter when I captured Bigfoot. I was completely unprepared and yet not only had I survived, I'd caught him singlehanded. Sure, there was a lot of dumb luck in that, but I still did it.

I suddenly sat bolt upright. I hadn't used two of the things that helped me the most last time: the tranquilizer gun and the net.

I slept like a baby that night, the plan forming in my head.

I made the phone call on the way to the park the next morning and gave specific instructions to The Man Who Doesn't Exist that there couldn't be any helicopters or anything the creature could spot. I gave the GPS coordinates for the nest and told him to wait for my signal.

I approached the clearing to the nest, tranquilizer gun out and ready, with a dozen more darts tucked away on a bandolier strapped across my chest. I gotta admit to feeling a little like I was in an old western.

As I hesitantly stepped into the open, I searched the skies. My eyes darted back and forth between the nest and the sky. Not knowing where it might come from, I turned back as well. Until I had reached the edge, I was nearly dizzy from looking all around like my head was on a swivel.

I paused for a moment to clear my head and regain my balance before stepping out onto the tree branch.

I took a deep breath as I took my second step. My eyes were locked on the nest. I knew I could no longer look around or I would lose my balance and plunge hundreds of feet to my gory death.

Wanting to avoid that, I stared straight ahead as I took another step and another. Soon I was halfway there and it was time to put my plan in action. I reached behind me and pulled out the net. I took a moment to balance myself, then threw the net over the nest.

That's what was supposed to happen. I was supposed to throw the net across the top of the nest, covering it and taking the creature's power of flight away so that it could easily be captured.

But unfortunately, that isn't what happened. My adrenaline was pumping so hard that I overshot and literally threw it *over* the nest.

I watched in horror and resignation as the net fluttered to the ground hundreds of feet below.

"Idiot!" I said.

My element of surprise gone; I went for broke. I stepped all the way to the nest and grabbed the side of it to keep from joining my net.

I held the gun out trying to acquire my target as quickly as possible.

What I saw made me decorate the inside of the nest with vomit.

The inside was covered with blood. Every part of it was red. Spread around the nest also were bones. There were so many bones I couldn't tell what any of them were, animal or human. And then I saw a backpack thrown to the side. It was ripped to pieces, but there was no doubt it belonged to a hiker.

As I was making my startling discovery, I heard wings flap.

I whipped around only to see a set of talons rushing toward my head. I ducked to avoid losing my face but, in the process, lost my balance. My arms pinwheeled but it wasn't enough, I had already gone past the tipping point and slowly stumbled off the branch into thin air.

The rushing air buffeted me as I plummeted to my death. I had stumbled off backward and was now falling backward, watching helplessly as the former safety of the branch retreated at terminal velocity.

I'd like to say my life flashed before my eyes, but it didn't. My future life flashed before me. All the things I could do with the millions I now had. I saw images of cars, mansions, and swimming pools full of women all fawning over me…

And then I was grabbed by my shoulders and lifted from my certain death.

I looked up preparing to thank the black-clad man with the parachute for saving me. But instead, I saw wings. My arms were held by talons. My savior was my enemy.

It flapped its wings hard sending us hurtling upward nearly as fast as I had fallen. I could see we were heading for the same place I had fallen from, the nest.

I panicked knowing exactly the fate that awaited me when we got to that pile of bones. My mind started running through options, but the fall and rescue was playing havoc with my common sense. By some miracle, I had held onto the tranquilizer gun the entire time. I pointed it at my captor but realized that would just kill us both.

We reached the nest, and it dropped me into the piles of bones. I must've landed wrong because I felt immediate pain in my side.

The creature landed and paced back and forth before screaming at me.

I pulled out the tranquilizer gun and shot it in the chest.

It screamed again as it stumbled then fell onto the bed of bones.

Men in black uniforms with no identifying patches on them appeared out of nowhere. They gathered the creature and took it to a clearing where a helicopter landed, picked them up, and took off all in less than a minute.

I was removed from the nest and taken to a clearing where The Man Who Doesn't Exist waited for me.

"Well done," he said extending his hand.

I shook it, wincing the whole time.

"You might want to get that taken care of. You have a broken rib."

"How can you tell that?"

He gently lifted my arm and showed a rib protruding from my side at a very strange angle.

"Oh my God," I said.

"It's not as bad as you think. It's not your rib."

He called a medic over and she examined the wound.

"It's not gonna be pretty," she said. "Hold on."

Then she grabbed the bone and ripped it out of my side.

My entire body exploded with pain. I fell to the ground thrashing in agony.

I saw a tranquilizer dart hit me in the chest. I glanced up and The Man was holding the gun.

"Take him to the hospital, patch him up, and get him home," he said just before the darkness took me.

I woke up in my bed, sat up, and felt a slight twinge of pain. I threw off my blanket and saw a small gauze patch on my side.

As I gazed around the room, I noticed a note on my bedstand next to a check with a lot of zeros on it.

The note read, 'Well done. You may want to take a few days off to let your wounds heal. PS, if you're going to spend money like you have been, you might want to use a plausible excuse for having said money. Maybe your rich uncle Murray you never knew named you in his will.

I look forward to your next call if you choose to continue.'

Chapter 3

I laid in bed for a day watching TV and generally healing my many wounds. The punctured lung was the worst. It wasn't severely punctured, just more like a scratched lung.

I made an anonymous phone call to the rangers and told them I had seen a huge bird carrying a bone that seemed like it might be human. I gave them the GPS coordinates and hung up. I made a bet with myself about which of my coworkers would jump on this information and try to take the credit for finding the hikers we'd been searching for. My money was on Jeff.

I had the TV on the entire time and my eye was caught by a show about rich people and how they live.

A thought suddenly struck me. I picked up my phone and within twenty-four hours I was lying on the deck of a rented yacht in the company of two lovely ladies. That was how I spent the rest of my vacation.

The second night I was awakened around 2 am. I peeled myself from between two sleeping women and got out of bed. I threw on a robe and stepped out onto the deck of the boat. The water shimmered with the moon being nearly full. We were anchored less than a mile from land, close enough to hear the waves crashing on the shore.

I scanned the horizon and listened for the sound that had woken me.

It wasn't long until I heard it. It was a long, mournful wail that seemed to call me towards it.

The park ranger and cryptid hunter in me begged to search out the source of the sound but I stood stoic, leaning against the rail, making no move whatsoever. Next, the park ranger and cryptid hunter demanded that I find out what that was, right now.

I told the voices to shut up. I was on vacation. Then I went back inside and fell into a deep sleep.

This went on for the rest of my time there. Every night I would hear the wail. Every night the voices would demand I chase it down. Every night I told them to shut the hell up.

It wasn't until I was flying home that I realized what an opportunity I had passed up, and how much I really didn't care.

When I got home it was the last day of my vacation. I spent the day setting up a dummy corporation for my money and buying some supplies for my cryptid hunting.

I had a backpack specially made with a parachute built into it so I wouldn't become the victim of a flying cryptid knocking me off a branch and nearly falling to my death... again. I also purchased more drones, another net, tasers, lots of tranquilizer darts, and some other specialty items. Lastly, I bought a new pickup with four doors and a cap on the back and loaded it with my equipment. It also had a bunk built, in case I got stuck out in the woods and had to camp for the night.

The following day I returned to the ranger station feeling refreshed but also depressed to be back in this environment.

I walked in the door and Nancy greeted me with a smile.

"Glad to see you back."

I turned to see who was behind me that she was talking to.

"How was your vacation?" she said.

"Not long enough," I said truthfully.

"Well, it hasn't been the same around here without you."

I was starting to wonder if this was the real Nancy or if I had found my next cryptid disguising itself as her.

"That's a nice truck you drove to work," she said. "Where'd you get the money for something like that?"

'There it is,' I thought. 'Just plain greed.'

"My rich uncle Murray passed away and left me a bundle," I said hoping the story would stick.

"Really? Maybe you could take me for a ride after work."

I ignored the double entendre while trying not to vomit at the thought.

"I'm pretty sure your husband wouldn't like that."

"What happens in the park stays in the park," she said raising her eyebrows.

It was too much. I had to walk away.

I went to my truck and drove off for my shift having no idea what monster/critter/cryptid I was gonna stumble upon next. I drove down by the lake and got out to enjoy the view. When I turned to go back to my truck I heard a large splash. I turned to see a huge expanding ripple in the water.

"You know what?" I said to the ripple. "Don't even mess with me because I am not equipped to handle you. You wanna hang out and give the tourists a thrill now and then be my guest. The rest of the time you just stay down in the muck at the bottom, so I don't have to see your ugly mug. Because if I see you then I'm gonna have to do something about you. So let's just pretend this didn't happen because I do not have the know-how or the firepower to take you down."

When I finished my diatribe, I noticed there was a woman in a jogging suit staring at me.

"Do you always talk to the lake?" she said eyeing me like I had just escaped the loony bin and dressed like a park ranger as a disguise.

"I wasn't talking to the lake. I was talking to the ripples."

She slowly backed away and continued her jog, shooting furtive looks back at me to make sure I wasn't following her. I was waiting for her to whip out her phone and call 911.

"Now look what you did," I said to the nearly vanished ripple. "Made me look crazy."

I shook my head and got back in my truck. As I did a few bubbles appeared on the surface where the ripples had been. I could swear I heard a very deep chuckle coming from the same spot. I resisted the urge to give the bubbles the finger because that would make me look even crazier.

I was about to pull away when I heard something off in the distance. I turned off the truck and listened closely. It was a long, mournful wail. In fact, it was the same as the one I'd heard on vacation.

It sent a chill down my spine but at the same time, it called to me. As if it was inviting me to join it.

My mind went into a major tizzy. Was this a similar creature to the one I'd heard so many thousand miles away, or more disturbingly, was this the same one? Following me all that way could only mean one thing… it was hunting me.

I pulled out my laptop and searched for cryptid sounds, more specifically the mournful wail. It came down to two possibilities, neither one was very good. Both used sound as a weapon against their victims. So, as usual, I went to town to pick up a specialty item I would need for my latest assignment.

Billy, the kid who seemed like he was always running the register, grinned when I walked in the door.

"What'll it be today?" he said. "A James Bond laser watch? A pen that lets you write in invisible ink underwater? Your own personal rocket ship?"

"I didn't inherit that much. How about some electronic noise-canceling earplugs?"

Billy scoffed. "That's not very exciting."

"I'm sorry to disappoint you," I said sarcastically.

"Try down on aisle seven for your earplugs."

"Thanks, Billy."

I strode down the surprising number of aisles for a local mom-and-pop store. It seemed like they had a little bit of everything sitting around waiting for someone to need it. It was like an island of misfit toys only for consumer products.

I searched aisle seven and found what I was looking for. They seemed like they'd been sitting around for I while, so I made sure to get some extra batteries to go with them.

Then I headed back to the park to search for my prey. I was pleasantly surprised by the comfort of the earplugs. That would make using them for extended periods of time much easier.

Of course, when I got back, I didn't hear the wailing anywhere. I drove through the entire park without hearing so much as a whimper.

I went home that night tired and frustrated. I decided to get a good night's sleep and come back fresh the next day.

The following day I hit the park early in search of my prey. I asked around with anyone I ran across. Hikers, campers, swimmers (yes, we have idiots that swim in our lake even though there's a, well… we have swimmers.) A few people had heard the sound and pointed me in the direction of it. Those who hadn't heard it gave me looks like I had gone coo-coo for coco puffs.

I used a map of the park and marked where I had talked to visitors and in which direction they had heard it. Slowly, after a few days of this, I began to narrow down the territory of this creature. Once I had a small enough area to look, I decided to camp out overnight and see if that didn't increase my chances of finding it.

I made sure I was the one who locked up, and then I just didn't leave. I locked myself and my truck in the park and drove to the area I thought had the best chance of success, and then I waited.

I found out a few things about myself as the time crept by like a sloth on valium. The biggest of which was that I'm not a patient person.

Playing games on my phone never held much interest to me. Reading a book was ok but as soon as I turned on a flashlight to see the pages, I was attacked by the mosquito swarm from hell.

I ended up sitting in the driver's seat with the windows rolled up so those thirsty little bloodsuckers couldn't get me. Not very conducive to tracking down sounds out in the woods.

So, after a two-can shower in disgusting bug spray, I was back outside. I even hosed down my flashlight, so they'd stay away from it. I considered picking a random direction and starting out but reconsidered. What use is it to bumble off through the woods when you don't even know where your prey is?

Just then I heard a mournful wail in the distance. My head snapped around like it was on a swivel and I zeroed in on the direction before loading up to pursue. I put on my backpack, then my utility belt that held my taser, pepper spray, and tranquilizer gun with extra darts.

I started walking feeling like a combination of a mountain climber and Batman. All I needed was a cowl.

"I'm Batman!" I said attempting to mimic his raspy voice but ending up in a coughing fit.

I started walking, not needing to be super quiet with all the crickets and birds and other nightly sounds so loud I had a hard time hearing the wail I was listening for.

I pulled out my phone and turned on the sound recorder. For a long few minutes, I stood still as the phone recorded the nightly sounds, and then finally the wail sounded again. It was closer this time and clearer. After the sound faded, I turned off my recorder and saved the sound.

I continued toward the general area where I heard the wail, adjusting my course every time I heard it. I knew I had to be closing in. At least I hoped so because I was quickly approaching the border between the park and private land.

In the park, a ranger is the ultimate authority. Yes, the power goes to my head sometimes, but this isn't about me. On the other side of the border on privately owned land, I'm subject to a buckshot enema if I step on the wrong property unannounced.

The sound pulled me right up to the border between public and private land. I stood at the borderline where a line of markers announced state park lands.

I glanced left and then right and saw no one, so I stepped out of my jurisdiction and into a place where I had no power. The trees weren't as thick, and I could see a small cottage off to the left that appeared like it may or may not be inhabited. It was a stone building and weeds grew up the outside with impunity.

I didn't see any lights on inside but then it was nearing midnight, and the occupant(s) could've been asleep. I did my best to keep it that way. Walking as quietly as possible past the house, never coming near enough to wake any sleeping dogs inside, (I hoped).

I heard the wail again and knew I was close. I went into stealth mode, stepping as quietly as possible while pulling out my tranquilizer gun and holding it ready.

The moon was only a thumbnail and didn't provide much light. I didn't want to use the flashlight this close and alert my prey to my presence, so I slowly pulled my night vision goggles out of my bag and put them on, bathing the world in an eerie green glow.

The creature wailed again. I was so close even the nightly noises didn't drown it out. I held the gun out in front of me, knowing I was close to danger and snuck up to a clearing. It had to be here. I aimed the gun with my night vision goggles making it look green like some alien weapon.

The wail echoed again right in front of me. I looked left and right but couldn't see anything making the sound. It had to be here. It was so loud.

'What the hell?' I thought. 'Is this thing invisible?'

I scanned back and forth, but all I could see were a couple of woodland creatures.

As I panned back through, I heard the sound again and happened to see something move at the same time. I focused on it and couldn't believe my eyes. I saw the creature that was wailing.

"Are you freaking kidding me?" I said as I ripped off my goggles and threw them down.

I put my gun back in its holster and kicked my expensive goggles in anger causing the creature to run away.

"A fox," I growled. "All this time I've been chasing a freaking fox!"

I tried to deny it but I knew it was the same sound I had heard before. My entire hunt had been for nothing. I hung my head and stood there for a few moments before turning to go back to my truck and call it a very unsuccessful night.

As I turned my face ran into the wrong end of a double-barrel shotgun.

At the other end of it was a woman who was a head shorter and several decades older than me.

"Evening, ranger," she said.

"Evening," I said back.

"You're a little out of your territory, aren't you?"

"Yes, ma'am," I said slowly raising my hands.

"This is private property."

"Yes, ma'am."

"My property."

"Yes, ma'am."

"What's all this ma'am business? You calling me old?"

"You're aiming a cannon at my face. I'll call you whatever you want."

She lowered the gun.

"What are you doing out here at this time of night anyways?"

"I got lost."

"Really? You expect me to believe that?"

"It's true," I said holding my best poker face.

She stepped over to my goggles and picked them up.

"You got lost with a pair of night vision goggles that probably cost more than your month's salary?"

"I recently got promoted."

"To what?"

"I'd rather not say."

Her eyes locked on mine. It felt as though she was probing my mind and reading every secret I've ever had.

"Ok," she said tossing me the goggles. "Well since you woke me up blundering through here, I'm going to have some tea. You want some?"

I knew the answer should be no. There was no way I should go into this person's house. I had no idea who she was or what she was capable of. I would be totally out of my mind to say…

"Sure, I'd like some tea."

I followed her back to the house I'd seen earlier and sat my pack outside by the door. I had to duck at the doorway to keep my head on my shoulders.

The inside was small but cozy. The room was lit entirely with candles sitting on the table, the mantle, and even a couple of wall fixtures. It bathed the room in a soft glow as if everything had a radiance exuding from it.

I smelled the scent of tea brewing wafting in from the kitchen. A few minutes later she came in holding two cups. I accepted one from her.

"Please sit," she said.

I lowered myself into a chair that didn't look very comfortable, however when I sat I melted into it. It may have been the most comfortable chair I'd ever sat in.

"So, tell me," she said sipping her tea. "What were you looking for out there tonight?"

"A fox of course."

She sipped again.

"I don't believe you were."

"Of course I was," I lied.

"That's why you were so disappointed that you kicked your expensive equipment?"

"It was the wrong color. I was looking for a grey fox instead of a red one."

"Hmm… " she said, taking another sip of tea, her eyes never leaving mine. "How much do park rangers make nowadays?"

"Oh, the same as usual."

"It's just you seem to have quite a bit of new and expensive equipment for a ranger."

"My uncle passed away and left me a sizable inheritance."

She smiled.

"We both know that's not true."

"Yes, it is."

"Whatever you say."

"It's true."

"Alright then, it's true," she said. "Who am I to know if someone's relative has passed or not?"

She sipped her tea.

"What about you?" I said.

"What about me?"

"Why are you out here in the middle of nowhere all by yourself?"

"I like it out here. I enjoy the woods and the animals. People leave me alone, for the most part."

She stared at me pointedly for the last part.

"I didn't come out here looking for you."

"Didn't you?" she said, her eyes shining in the candlelight.

My breath caught in my throat.

"No," I said unsure if I believed it or not.

"You're not a park ranger are you," she said looking over the rim of her cup.

"Of course I… "

"No, you may have been once. But now you're something… else."

Either her voice or the chair or the candles, hell maybe all three, had me in a daze. I could feel myself being carried off to a land of sweet slumber. My mind was screaming at me to wake up and get out. With supreme effort, I rose from my chair and set the cup on the table. My hand hovered over the pistol.

"This has been a very interesting visit, but I think it's time for me to leave."

"Yes, of course," she said setting her tea down and standing.

She offered her hand and I stared at it for a long moment before shaking it.

"Maybe we'll run across each other some other time," she said.

"Maybe we will," I said before ducking my head through the doorway and out into the evening air.

The coolness hit me right away. It wasn't just the temperature; it was like I had just broken free from some mental web.

I didn't hear the wail again that night as I retrieved my pack, made my way back to my truck, and left the park. My mind was preoccupied as I drove home. Who was that woman? What was that woman?

The next day as I was walking through the park someone snuck up behind me.

"Hello there, ranger," she said.

I nearly jumped out of my skin and did a comical dance trying not to fall down.

She laughed as I composed myself.

"Are you trying to scare me to death?" I said fighting back some of the other words I wanted to say.

"Not just yet."

I hesitated.

"When?" I said quietly.

"Don't worry. You'll have plenty of time to spend your 'inheritance'... I think."

I shot her a look.

"Who are you?"

"If you want to know the truth don't start with a lie. Who are you?"

"I think you already know who I am," I said. "Or do you want to hear the words?"

"The words would be nice," she said her grey robe and hair flowing in the breeze.

I glanced left and right to be sure no one was close enough to hear.

"Cryptid hunter," I said. "Your turn."

"Excuse me for answering a question with a question, but what were you chasing last night? What did you think you were going to find?"

"I wasn't sure," I said honestly. "I'm never sure what I'll find when I go looking."

"And yet you go anyway? Not knowing and maybe not caring about the possible danger you could be walking into?"

I shrugged. "I've been ok so far."

She stared at me as serious as a heart attack.

"Don't you think that someday dumb luck might run out?"

"That's when I fall back on technology," I said patting the taser in its holster.

She smiled ruefully. "I've never put much faith in technology. It's very cold and impersonal."

"You still haven't told me who you are."

"You're right," she said, then turned and walked away.

She stopped and faced me.

"If you want to know who I am be at my house tonight at midnight."

"Midnight? Really?"

"I'll see you then."

She stepped around the corner in the trail and disappeared. I ran around the corner to see her but she was nowhere to be found.

The rest of the day was a blur as I watched the clock incessantly. I became convinced that midnight would never come. As if somewhere, someone was holding up Moses' arms so the sun would stay in place.

As my excitement built so did my dread. Out in the middle of nowhere, I'd be on my own. Her comments about dumb luck running out and death still burned in my mind. If this was the creature I thought it was I could be pushing up daisies tomorrow, even if she did look like a kindly old woman.

As the clock struck eleven, I decided to enlist some insurance.

At midnight I sat in my truck on the dirt road that ran in front of her house.

She stepped out and motioned for me to come in.

I kept my utility belt on as I got out of the truck. I may be stupid but I ain't dumb. Going in there without a weapon of some sort would be a new kind of crazy.

I ducked inside her doorway to the room looking the same as yesterday. The only thing that I hadn't noticed before was a stuffed crow on the mantle. At least I thought it was stuffed. It had those eyes that seemed to follow you everywhere.

I sat in the same comfortable chair as she handed me a cup of tea. While she turned to go to her seat, I gave it a quick sniff.

"Don't worry," she said without looking. "I didn't put anything in the tea."

I took a quick sip and then set it down on the table. She settled into her chair and fixed me with a look.

"So, you want to know who I am," she said.

I nodded like a little kid being asked questions by the teacher.

"But you must have some idea, or you wouldn't be here."

"You made me tell you I was a cryptid hunter."

"And how exactly does that work?" she said with an edge in her voice. "Do you kill them?"

"What? No, of course not. They're way too valuable for that."

She sat back as if the answer had surprised her.

"What does happen?"

"I capture the creature then call up some people and they come to get it."

"And give you a considerable sum for it."

I shrugged. "Of course."

Her eyes penetrated mine as she leaned forward.

"Have you ever considered that these creatures don't want to leave their home?"

"I actually have," I lied leaning forward. "Have you ever stood knee-deep in the blood and bones of the victims of one of these creatures? I have."

She sat back.

"Really?" she said. "Animal bones?"

"Mixed with human."

"And which do you consider more important?"

"Human of course," I said. "But these creatures are all apex predators. Every creature has the right to hunt but when you have one that is at the top of the food chain, they need to be kept in check."

"Like humans? Am I an apex predator?"

"No," I said trying to keep my voice from shaking. "You're something more than that."

"And therefore, I must be caged."

I lowered my head and pulled out my tranquilizer gun.

"I'm sorry. I've already called and told them I was on the hunt and if they didn't hear from me by 1 o'clock to zero in on my GPS signal and come to the rescue."

Her eyes shone with sadness. She gave no resistance as I aimed the gun at her. This time there was no haziness in my mind. No sleepiness tugged at the corners of my consciousness. She was allowing me the choice of taking her.

Pulling the trigger seemed impossible. My mind was screaming at me not to do it.

She watched my internal struggle.

"What if I could offer you an alternative?" she said.

"I'm listening."

I drove her to the lake and unlocked the gate. I parked the truck near the water and sat waiting.

"Are you sure this'll work?" I said.

"I'm betting my freedom on it."

She smiled and got out of the truck. "Just remember… " she said pointing to my ears.

"I know."

She stepped away from the truck and to the edge of the lake. She closed her eyes and started singing. It was a beautiful yet discordant melody. I knew it would never hit the top 40.

She raised her arms as the melody poured out of her, washing over the surface of the lake and causing all other sounds to cease.

Her song ended and she stood as still as a statue, waiting.

A few moments later the water stirred. A head broke through the surface and peered around as though looking for any prying eyes.

A beautiful woman with long hair covering her chest and fish scales from her waist down emerged from the water and spoke to the old woman.

"I told you never to call me again," the lake woman said.

"I wanted to make peace."

The woman laughed.

"Make peace? There is no peace to be made between you and I. Depart before I foretell of *your* demise."

"I have an offering," the old woman said gesturing toward the truck.

On cue, I got out and approached.

The lake woman eyed me up and down.

"This offering is good, but it's not enough. Bring me one of these each night for a month and I'll consider your petition."

The old woman bowed her head in acquiescence as the lake woman approached me. She began to sing, and I swooned. She turned and started back into the lake with me following behind, captive to her song. I struggled against the tugging I felt. The earplugs were working, mostly, but I still faltered, my hand hovering over the gun.

With a supreme effort, I pulled out my gun and shot a dart into her back. She turned and hissed at me as her beautiful face morphed into a hideous monster. Her eyes narrowed unnaturally, and her teeth grew longer and sharper. She lunged at me but missed and fell face-first into the lake a victim of the sedative.

I pulled her out of the water and slung her over my shoulder. As I turned toward the truck she used her last ounce of energy to bite me.

"Ow, dammit!" I said dropping her on the shore.

"Let me see," the old woman said.

"It's not fatal, is it?" I said half joking.

She slapped my shoulder playfully.

"No, it's not fatal. Jerk."

I smiled as I pulled out my phone.

"You should probably go."

She reached up and kissed my cheek.

"Thank you," she said walking away.

"Back atcha," I said holding my shoulder as I watched her disappear.

Within ten minutes The Man Who Doesn't Exist was standing in front of me as the black-clad men with no identifying patches took the creature. A medic was tending to my wound.

"Not as bad as last time," she said shooting me a smile.

"Thanks, I'll try to do better."

The Man Who Doesn't Exist shook my hand.

"Well done," he said. "I saw you set up a dummy corporation. Very smart. I'll wire the money to it."

"Thanks," I said pulling my shirt over the bandage on my wound.

"Anything else you have for me?" he said scanning the area.

"How many were you expecting?" I chuckled. "Am I supposed to up my quota?"

His eyes bore into mine for a long moment as I held my breath.

"Of course not. You've done well."

"Thanks."

"Until next time," he said getting into the helicopter and flying away.

"Yeah," I said rubbing my shoulder. "Next time."

Chapter 4

I stood by the edge of the lake watching the helicopter fly away. I was amazed at how quiet it was. I assumed it was some kind of stealth technology.

I rubbed my injured shoulder and wished I could take another vacation. 'Maybe I could fake an injury or sickness,' I thought, imagining another month in the arms of two lovely ladies as we stared out over glistening clear water. 'But that wouldn't work if one of my idiot coworkers came to visit me in the hospital. In fact, now that they know I have money, that's a distinct possibility.'

I sighed. 'I guess I'll just have to wait for the weekend like everybody else. I'm sure I can fly away and pack a lot of fun into forty-eight hours.'

I turned away from the lake and headed back to my truck as a large splash sounded from the water.

I stopped and sighed.

"Not today," I said without turning around.

I drove home and collapsed in my bed, exhausted yet I couldn't get that woman out of my head. Sleep came eventually and fitfully. When my alarm went off, I nearly cried. I felt like I'd been run over by a truck.

I glanced at my watch.

'Dammit, it's only Wednesday,' I thought. 'Maybe I'll take Friday off and fly away for a three-day weekend.'

I checked my bank account and found no deposit. I was about to go full hissy fit when I remembered what he had said and checked the account of my dummy corporation.

I sighed with relief seeing the account had grown by the usual amount.

I showered, dressed, and headed for work grabbing a quick breakfast and coffee on the way.

I had barely made it to the front door of the station when I was accosted by Jeff.

"There he is," Jeff said grabbing me in a bear hug and making me wince in pain. "I haven't seen you around much. How have we been missing each other?"

"Just luck I guess," I said trying not to scream.

"Such a kidder," Jeff said releasing me. "You missed all the reporters when I broke the missing hikers' case."

'What a shock,' I thought. 'Jeff took credit for it. Who would've called that?'

"Too bad," I said. "I guess you're some kind of hero now. Maybe I don't deserve to be in your presence."

"Aw no. I haven't let it go to my head."

'That's why you're mentioning it a month later,' I thought.

"Well, I better get out there," I said. "Those hikers aren't gonna rescue themselves."

Nancy and Jeff followed me out like stray dogs.

I got into my truck and drove away, not looking back. Once I was out of sight, I let out a sigh.

'I guess I need to get some anti-suck-up medicine somewhere.'

I started my regular route down by the lake. When no hikers came running up to me to say that one of their relatives had managed to get lost or eaten, I went over to the spot where I had caught my first cryptid.

Strangely enough, no one had removed the bear trap. It wasn't set, but still, it was weird. I'd have to talk to the person in charge of investigating how that trap got there. Oh, wait, that would be me.

As I chuckled to myself, I had a strange feeling that something was wrong. The birds had suddenly stopped singing. The silence was eerie.

I turned around and there stood another creature like the first one I'd captured. It wasn't quite as tall as the first and it had bumps on its chest. It was also glaring at me and snarling.

I quickly put two and two together.

"H… Hello, Mrs. umm… Foot," I said letting my hand slowly drift down toward my tranq gun. "I'll bet you're wondering where your husband is."

She let out a massive roar that nearly made me pee my pants.

"Absolutely, you have every right to be upset. I'd be upset too if my husband ran off with some hot Werewolf like that."

My hand was nearly to my gun when she'd had enough. She lunged at me, slashing at my hand, and knocking the gun away. I screamed in pain and grabbed for my taser. She swatted that away too then aimed another slash at me. It would've hit me in the throat, but I tripped as I was backpedaling away, and it ended up ripping across my side.

I lay on the ground defenseless and bleeding. She came at me again. I reached painfully around to my backpack trying to find anything that I could use as a weapon. As I tugged at the zipper my hand slipped and I pulled the release for the parachute.

It sprung out and flopped onto the ground. She paused staring at the white material then resumed her assault. I tried to use the time to get away. I struggled to my feet and started running. Suddenly I was yanked backward. I turned and found Mrs. Bigfoot holding the parachute chords and dragging me toward her.

I couldn't tell for sure out of sheer terror what would happen when she finished reeling me in like the catch of the day, but I thought I saw her smiling.

I pulled out my cell phone and dialed The Number.

"Yes," said The Man Who Doesn't Exist.

"Help me!" I screamed.

He didn't hesitate.

"I can be there in ten minutes."

"I don't think there'll be anything left by then!"

The line disconnected.

I couldn't decide if that was good news because he was hurrying to help me or bad news because he was sick of my shit and was sitting back to have a cup of tea while Mrs. Bigfoot dined on my entrails. In either case, I figured I should try to avoid the latter if possible.

She nearly had me. There was only one thing I could think of doing. I jumped up and dove inside the parachute.

I was instantly blind being surrounded by material but kept crawling as far as I could away from the furball of death.

I could feel the parachute being pulled. She was using the same tactic as before, reeling me in, only this time I had the element of surprise. I pulled out my hunting knife and sliced a hole in the chute. As soon as I saw daylight, I jumped out and cut the chute cords. I then gathered them up and started towards the monster struggling through the chute.

It appeared as if the chute was fighting itself. The white material was being thrown around by a monster under it. It was like a ghost on crack having a psychotic episode. It would've been funny if my life wasn't on the line.

I grabbed the chute cord and started making laps around the struggling ghostly figure. As I wrapped around it, the fight became more violent. I started taking wide laps around her with the cord making very sure to stay out of reach. I started low and wrapped a few laps around her legs, then went high trying to limit her arm movements.

For her part, she howled and punched and swung at the parachute that enveloped her, but there was nothing tangible for her to hit. I was amazed she hadn't used her claws yet when four holes punctured through the material and ripped all the way to the ground.

She stepped out of her nylon prison and turned to find me.

Her lips curled up in a vicious snarl as she shed the material and started toward me.

I once again gave serious thought to why I was still endangering myself cryptid hunting when I had over a hundred million dollars to my name.

She flexed her claws as she advanced on me.

"I feel this would be a good time for me to apologize. I'm a big enough man to admit when I was wrong. I'm sure you don't hear that very much, a guy admitting he was wrong, but here I am."

Nothing I said had slowed her approach in the slightest.

"I'm sorry I drugged your husband," I said slowly backing away from her. "And dropped him off a ledge into the truck, and flopped him onto concrete, and nudged him into the storage unit with the bumper of my truck and sold him like a prize steer. It was purely accidental."

She had reached striking distance and I had backed into a tree.

"No hard feelings?" I said extending my hand.

She extended her claws and reared back for the killing stroke.

I knew I was done.

I closed my eyes and thought of lounging on the deck of the boat with those two lovely ladies surrounded by calm, clear, blue water.

Regret punched me in the face and told me I was an idiot.

I wasn't looking forward to death, especially not at the hands of Bigfoot's estranged, deranged wife, but it seemed like she was taking a long time to finish me off.

I peeked one eye open and saw her standing there, frozen, with her arm reaching back about to strike.

I marveled at this apparition with morbid curiosity when she fell over like a redwood tree.

Behind her, holding a nasty-looking taser, was The Man Who Doesn't Exist, along with several of his unmarked soldiers.

I slid down the tree and slumped forward. Feeling more gratitude than I had since, well, since the last time they rescued me.

"Did you guys stop for coffee?"

The Man glanced at his watch.

"It's been nine minutes and thirty-five seconds since your call."

I chuckled.

"I'm glad you were early."

"Are you injured?"

I raised my arm painfully and showed him my shredded uniform that was red and getting redder.

"Let's get you to a hospital," he said as two soldiers gently lifted me.

They took me over to the helicopter and the female medic gave me a quick once over.

"I thought I told you to be safe?" she said as she checked my wounds.

"Sorry, I'll try to make my next visit less injure-y."

She smiled and sprayed something on me that made me wince.

"Sorry, but I don't want to bandage it since they'll just rip it off at the hospital to see the injury anyway."

I crawled into the helicopter as I saw them loading Mrs. Foot in the other one. I told The Man the story on the trip to the hospital.

"It seems you have creatures coming to you now," he said with a sideways grin.

"Well maybe I can set up an iron cage for an office and they can schedule a time to come meet with me. Then I can just slip out the back door."

He chuckled.

"If anyone could get away with that, I think it would be you."

We landed a mile away from the hospital where the medic changed into civilian clothes and put me in a car that was waiting for us. She drove me to the hospital posing as my girlfriend and took me to the counter before 'remembering' she needed to park the car.

I gave her a slight nod as she walked out the door.

They treated my wounds and told me they were deep but no ribs were broken. They made me spend the night 'for observation'. Which I knew meant, 'so we can get more money from the insurance company for you just lying around in one of our beds'.

I wish I had thought up a racket like that. I'd be a quintillionaire instead of just a lowly millionaire.

Speaking of money, my phone dinged. I read the text, 'Money delivered, usual amount.'

I texted back, 'Keep it, for saving my life.'

There was a long pause before the reply, 'I genuinely appreciate the gesture, but no, you've earned it.'

'Tell Mrs. Foot I hope she won't be too hard on her husband. Lol.'

'I'll be sure to pass along the message.' There was a smiley face emoji.

I chuckled. Then put my phone down, laid back, and focused on not being in excruciating pain.

A few hours later I woke to smiling faces. Nancy, Jeff, Ron, Sharon, and even Dell my boss were all standing around my bed having a 'let's see who can smile the biggest' competition, except for Dell.

"Hey," I said.

"How are you feeling," they all said at the same time making them sound like some weird chorus.

"Umm… good."

Nancy jumped to the front of the pack and spoke first.

"We heard you'd been attacked. What was it?"

I thought for a long moment.

"I'm not sure," I lied. "It happened so fast. I think it was a mountain lion."

"Well, I'm glad you're safe," Jeff said pushing to the front.

"I'm glad he's safe too," Sharon said trying to jostle for position.

"Yeah," Don said, shoving. "Super glad."

Dell just shook his head.

"Back off you idiots. You want him to suffocate before you can suck any money out of him?"

They all backed up and turned on Dell with wounded expressions but none of them said a word.

"I guess this means you'll be taking more sick time," Dell said.

"Sorry my injuries are such an inconvenience to you," I said.

He stared at me.

"Yeah, well let me know when you plan to come back," he said turning to leave.

"Tomorrow," I called after him. "I'll be back on the job tomorrow."

He paused and nodded, then left.

They all turned and stared at me.

"What was that about?"

"None of your business," I said. "Now the rest of you can clear out too."

My bed was surrounded by wounded expressions.

"Don't you people have jobs?" I said. "Git!"

Then I turned away and stared out the window. One by one they straggled out. Nancy lingered but I refused to make eye contact and she left too.

I more felt than heard someone step back into the room and linger. I could tell it wasn't a nurse.

"I thought I told you… " I said turning and facing the old woman I'd just saved from capture.

"Told me what?" she said.

"Sorry, I thought you were someone else."

"May I come in?" she said standing at the doorway.

"Of course," I said. "Unless you're here as a messenger."

She smiled.

"Not yet."

I relaxed without realizing I'd tensed up.

She stepped over to my bedside and sat in the chair.

"I'm surprised to see you," I said. "I didn't think our paths would cross again after I nearly sent you to a cryptid zoo."

"That definitely would've put a damper on our relationship," she said. "However, you didn't and I'm grateful for that."

"And what exactly is our relationship?"

She shrugged.

"What would you like it to be?"

"How about friendship?" I said.

She smiled.

"Friendship sounds good."

"Friendship requires trust."

"It certainly does."

"And trust requires I know a thing or two."

"Such as?"

"Such as your name."

She paused and stared at me.

"No one has asked my name in a long time."

"Why?" I said. "Does it make you lose power or something?"

"You read too much science fiction," she said. "No, I just haven't talked to many people in the last few years."

"Yeah, you don't exactly live on main street," I said. "So how about that name?"

"Oh, right, it's Dolores."

"Dolores?"

"Yes," she said. "Do you have a problem with Dolores?"

"No. It's just not what I would expect for a… " I paused and glanced around to make sure no one was listening. "Banshee."

She smiled.

"And how many Banshees do you know?"

"Currently, one."

"What did you expect my name to be?"

"I don't know, something weird and mysterious I guess," I said. "Something unpronounceable, like the human tongue was unable to make the sound."

"Nope, It's Dolores."

"Ok," I said. "So what brings you by, Dolores?"

"I need your help."

"What's the problem?"

"I have something that's getting after my animals."

"You want me to come and chase off a coyote for you?"

"Do you have something better to do? Is there some pressing engagement on your social calendar?"

"I'll have to check with my secretary," I said sarcastically.

"Alright, well have her people call my people and set up a meeting," she said getting up. "In the meantime, get some rest."

I watched her glide out of the room wearing that same grey robe that flowed so regally.

I laid my head back and reflected on how strange my life had become recently. Eventually, I nodded off to sleep.

When morning came, I checked myself out of the hospital against medical advice. They wanted me to stay longer but I had better things to do, and I had no desire to give them one more cent. I was more tempted to buy the place and bulldoze it. Maybe hire a half dozen doctors to go back to the way it used to be when doctors went to see their patients instead of making sick people travel dozens or hundreds of miles to be cheated out of their life savings.

But I digress.

I don't know how he did it, but The Man had my truck parked in the hospital lot right up front. When I stepped up into it my side hurt a bit. I would have to take it easy.

I didn't bother going to the station. I had no desire to deal with all the suckups. I did a round and ended up at Dolores's place. Parking alongside the road didn't seem too obtrusive when mine would probably be the only vehicle on it all day.

I stepped up to her door and went to knock but the door opened. I stepped in and ducked through her doorway.

"Ah, you made it," she said coming out of the kitchen as the door closed behind me. "Welcome back to the land of the living."

I turned to the door, then back to her, a question lingering on my lips, but I decided to leave well enough alone.

"So, where's this thing that's getting after your animals?" I said.

"Listen to you, all business," she said carrying two cups into the living room. "Sit down and have some tea."

"I'm on duty."

"Like that's stopped you before."

"Touché'," I said dropping into the incredibly comfortable chair. "It's not like I'm a real park ranger anymore."

I sipped the tea and was impressed with its flavor.

"How's your boss?"

"Dell? He's an asshole. He erased my first bigfoot pictures off my phone."

"That's not surprising," she said. "But that's not the boss I'm talking about."

"You mean The Man Who Doesn't Exist?"

She nodded.

"We go back a ways," she said. "I'm sure he'd love to have me as a 'guest' in his little zoo."

"I won't turn you in if that's what you're asking."

"There may come a time when he won't give you the choice."

"We have an open agreement, he and I. I bring him whatever I find, no questions asked."

"For now," she said sipping her tea.

I sat silently pondering her puzzling predicament when I heard an animal outside calling in distress.

"Ah, just in time," she said rising and heading toward the back of the house.

I got up and followed her. We peered out a window to an open field where an animal was being attacked by what looked like something out of a horror movie. It was the size of a large dog, but it had spines on it like a dinosaur. It was trying to bring down a goat that was running in circles to avoid it.

"What the hell is that?" I said.

"A Chupacabra."

"An Oompa loompa?"

"Chupacabra," she corrected.

I pulled out my tranq gun.

"That won't work," she said like she was chiding a child for a wrong decision. "Its hide is too thick and leathery. It has its own armor."

I put the tranq gun back in its holster and reached for my taser.

"That won't work either," she said.

"What am I supposed to use?" I said frustrated. "I didn't get my parachute reloaded yet to use as a weapon."

"You used a parachute as a weapon?"

"Long story," I said. "Suffice it to say Mrs. Bigfoot will probably never look at a parachute the same way again."

"I'd like to hear that story someday," she said. "But now back to our friend."

"The chimichanga?"

"Chupacabra," she patiently corrected.

I wracked my brain until I saw it had the goat on the ground and was going in for the kill. Without thinking I ran out the back door and started yelling at it and waving my arms. The creature was startled and ran away.

"That's fine for the moment," Dolores said. "But it'll be back."

"I hope so," I said. "Help me get the goat up."

"Why?"

"We need to guide it into my truck."

"I don't understand."

"Trust me, I have a plan."

Fifteen minutes later the goat sat unhappily in the back of my truck. Dolores and I sat in the front seat while I held the rope we'd tied around the goat's neck to keep it from running off.

"I still don't see how this is going to work," she said.

"It's simple, the back door is open, the goat makes noise and draws in the candelabra… "

"Chupacabra."

"Whatever, it comes in through the back door, we pull the goat through the front hatch and shut it while I go around and shut the back door. Easy peasy."

"What could possibly go wrong?" she said rolling her eyes.

"I know, right?"

We sat and waited for a long time. The goat even got bored and lay down.

"Come on," I said after a while. "What do I have to do, lure it in with a trail of Scooby snacks?"

Just then the truck jostled a little. I looked in the rear-view mirror and saw it sneaking up on the goat. I slid out of the truck as quietly as possible and snuck around to the back. I slammed the back door shut and ran back to the front to a horrible scene. The creature had come through the hatch with the goat and now Doloras, the goat, and the creature were all fighting for their lives.

I wanted to open the door and help but didn't know what I could do when suddenly my ears were assaulted. I slammed my hands against the side of my head as Doloras let out the loudest, most piercing scream I've ever heard.

Both the animals were instantly incapacitated.

She climbed out of the truck as I climbed in. I shoved the creature into the back and shut the door, then pulled the trembling goat out of the front. I laid it on the ground and then went to check on Dolores.

"Are you ok?" I said.

She was breathing hard and fell into my arms. I caught her and carried her inside the house where I laid her down on the couch. I went to the kitchen and poured a cup of tea then brought it to her.

"So, this is what you do for a living," she said examining the scratches on her arms.

"Fun, huh?" I said.

"Not so much."

"Are you gonna be alright?"

She took the tea and sipped a little.

"I'll be fine," she said. "You should go take your prize to your friend before that thing destroys your truck."

"What about you?"

She smiled weakly.

"I'll be fine," she said. "I think I'll take a nap."

"You're sure?"

"Yes, don't fret over an old woman."

I rose and glanced at her wounds. They didn't seem as bad as they had a minute ago.

"If you're sure… "

"Get out of here," she said.

"I'll be back to check on you later," I said stepping toward the door.

She smiled.

"Thanks for taking care of my problem."

I smiled back.

"Anytime, ma'am," I said and pretended to tip a hat.

As I stepped out the goat wandered past me. I chuckled as I turned toward my truck which looked like it was having convulsions. Apparently, the critter had woken up and wasn't happy with his current accommodations.

I got into the cab that was ripped to pieces and reeked like a dog had died in it then drove to a secluded area on the other side of the park before calling The Man.

They showed up with their usual promptness, removed the creature, and were on their way.

The Man smiled at me.

"I didn't expect to hear from you for a while," he said looking me over. "And relatively uninjured this time."

I shrugged.

"What can I say? I'm a machine."

He eyed me curiously.

"Did you have help?"

I met his gaze.

"Would it be a problem if I did?"

"Not at all," he said. "I was just curious as to who."

I smiled.

"Someone who wishes to remain anonymous."

He nodded and shook my hand.

"Fair enough."

The medic looked at me.

"Are trying to make me obsolete?" she said.

"Perish the thought," I said kissing her hand. "I'll always need you to take care of me."

She smiled and stepped into the helicopter with The Man.

They flew off nearly silent leaving me standing next to my ruined truck. I looked in the back and saw all my equipment destroyed. I sighed, then a thought struck me. I drove to the station and found all the rangers inside.

"Hey, Nancy, remember that ride you wanted to take?" I said.

"Yeah."

"Here you go," I said tossing her the keys. "It's yours."

"Really?" she said.

"You deserve it."

She looked around the room at the other rangers and strutted out of the station dangling the keys with a smug look on her face.

I hopped into my old ranger truck and watched as she walked up to the truck and saw the damage. Her jaw dropped open as she did a slow lap around the ruined truck. When she opened the door, she covered her nose and retched.

I drove home laughing all the way.

Chapter 5

When I was a kid if you would've told me that when I grew up, I would hunt monsters for a living, I would've said you were crazy. Of course, when I was a kid if you would've told me Spiderman wasn't real, I probably would've said you were crazy too.

It's funny what we convince ourselves of. I thought these thoughts as I lay in bed nursing sore ribs and an injured shoulder. The ribs from a crazed female bigfoot who was out for revenge because I took her husband away and the shoulder from a siren that bit me as a last act of revenge before she was carted off.

It sounded crazy even to me. Let's not even get into the man who shows up with his private army in black stealth helicopters to take away these creatures and gives me millions of dollars for it.

Yes, my life had been some kind of crazy since I decided to hunt down that first creature. But it was nothing compared to what was to come…

I looked at my watch.

'Dammit!' I thought. 'Time to go to work.'

I got up, swallowed some painkillers with some old coffee and drove to the car dealership to order a new truck. Then I stopped in at the local store to pick up some basic supplies and a prepaid cell phone. I knew it would make me late to work and my boss would be mad, but I didn't care. Surprisingly, Billy wasn't at the checkout to make some smart remark.

"Where's Billy?" I asked the cashier.

"He's off today," she answered.

"I'm surprised," I said. "Seems like every time I'm in here he's working."

"I think he works a second job at a restaurant," she said. "You know how bills are."

"Yeah," I said knowing full well that I would never have to worry about bills again.

I paid for my items and left, then drove to the park with Billy on my mind.

'Maybe I should have an assistant,' I thought. 'Eventually one of these things is gonna get lucky and take out the one hunting it. I would rather that not be me. An assistant to throw into the mouth of danger… I mean to help me out, would be nice.'

The rest of the way to work one word kept rattling through my head… 'sidekick'.

I pulled into the station at the same time Nancy did. She was in her ratty old Toyota.

"Hey, Nancy, what happened to that new truck you just got?" I said smiling ear to ear.

She slammed her car door shut and walked into the station without looking at me. I knew she wanted to tell me off but wouldn't risk killing the cash cow.

When we walked into the station, Dell was right up in our faces.

"So, you both feel like you're too good to show up to work on time?" he said.

"I had car trouble," Nancy said, shooting me a dirty look.

"I just don't care," I said, shooting Dell an arrogant smirk.

"I should fire you," he said stepping up nose to nose with me. Which was especially funny since he was a few inches shorter.

"Go for it," I said making sure to pronounce the 't' strong enough that spittle flew in his face.

We stood in a silent standoff as Nancy took advantage of the situation and snuck off.

"My office," Dell said, turning and marching away.

I followed so closely that I stepped on the back of his shoe and gave him a flat tire.

I chuckled as he almost fell trying to put the heel back in his shoe while still storming to his office.

When we got there, I walked around and sat in his chair as he was slamming the door.

When he turned around and saw me in his chair with my feet on his desk his face turned a special kind of red. I called it, 'Too pissed off to breathe' red.

He took a moment to settle down then leaned over the desk with his knuckles on it.

"I don't give a damn how much money you have I will not see you make a mockery of this station," he said.

"Oh, you mean with people like Jeff and Nancy who couldn't get jobs as garbage collectors?"

"This isn't about them, it's about you," he said.

"What about me? I come to work, do my job, go home. How is that an embarrassment?"

"I know what you're doing. I've seen you going around hunting those things."

"Oh really?" I said leaning on the desk right in front of his knuckles. "I thought those things didn't exist. Isn't that what you told me when you deleted the pictures off my phone? You told me to take the day off and get my head clear. Well, my head is clear, and my bank account is healthier than it's ever been. So, you tell me, who's right and who's wrong?"

He stood there silently fuming, turning that special shade of red.

"How about we do this?" I said. "You shut the hell up and pretend you're a real boss, and I'll keep doing what I do."

I didn't wait for his answer. I walked around the end of the desk and left the room nearly knocking over the three rangers that were standing just outside the door trying to hear what was going on.

I stepped through them, ignoring their questions, and walked out, then drove straight to Dolores' house and knocked on the door. It opened and I stormed in.

As usual, she was nowhere near the door when it shut on its own. She ambled out of a side room and gave me a look.

"You seem quite out of sorts," she said gliding to the kitchen.

I plopped into my favorite chair in a huff.

"My boss is giving me a hard time," I said.

"Which one?"

"Not the one who pays me lots of money."

"Really? I thought you would just ignore the other one, seeing how you really don't need that job anymore."

"It makes a nice cover."

"Then what's the problem?"

"He still thinks I'm going to jump through his hoops like everyone else and I'm not."

"Hmm… " she said, handing me a cup of tea. "So, you don't like being controlled and he doesn't like not being able to control you. Sounds like a dilly of a pickle."

I laughed in spite of myself.

"How old are you again?"

"Let's not make this personal, there sonny boy," she said, waggling a finger playfully at me.

I let out a long breath.

"I guess it's also getting to me because I've been having second thoughts."

"About this strange career path that you're on?"

"Yeah, how many cryptid hunters make it to retirement?"

"I'm not sure," she said. "If you're looking for job security, I think you're in the wrong business."

"That's what I'm afraid of."

I took a sip of tea and enjoyed the warmth sliding down my throat, soothing me into a calmer attitude.

"What do you think I should do?"

"Why ask me?" she said, sipping her own tea.

"Well first of all because we're friends," I said. "And second because you're… "

She shot me a warning look.

"… more experienced than I am."

"Nice save," she said.

"Thanks."

"Let me put it this way," she said. "You see this house? This is me. This is who I am. This is all I want to be. If someone were to shower me with more money than I could possibly spend I would still be here in this house. I wouldn't change who I am. I might take a lot more trips than I do, but other than that, I would still be me."

"I get it," I said. "That's probably why I stayed a park ranger. It's who I am. I suck at it, but it's who I am."

"No, it's not," she said leaning forward. "Your job doesn't define you. You define you. You enjoy your job but you aren't your job. You have to be you in order to be happy."

"Wow, that's deep," I said.

"You like that?" she said. "I got it from a fortune cookie."

I laughed.

"So, while I'm having an existential crisis, you're making jokes," I said. "Remind me again why we're friends."

She leaned forward and took my hand.

"Because I remind you that life is more than it appears on the surface."

"Ok, that really is deep," I said. "If you're gonna keep talking like this I'm gonna need something stronger than tea."

"No need," she said, leaning back. "I'm done."

I scrunched down into my chair and rested my head on the back.

"Maybe I should take a little break."

"Thinking of another vacation?"

"Always, but that's not what I'm talking about," I said. "I know the deck is stacked against me with this cryptid-hunting gig. I also know that I've cheated death a few times already."

"True enough," she said. "I've come close to singing your song."

"So, bringing on an assistant doubles my odds of survival."

"That's true," she said, eyeing me cautiously. "Who did you have in mind?"

"There's a kid that works at a local store in town."

"A kid?" she said.

"Yeah, not an actual kid, he's in his early twenties, I think, why?"

"No reason."

"No really, I value your opinion, if there's a problem you see let's hear it."

She sighed.

"I thought you were going to ask me."

I laughed.

"Oh, no, that never entered my mind."

Her lips thinned and she shot up out of the couch like a spring and stormed off to the kitchen.

I got up and followed her.

"What's wrong?" I said, as she slammed teacups around breaking one.

"You, that's what's wrong," she said sticking her finger in my face. "You think I'm too old and feeble to help you. Who do you think took care of that Chupacabra without your help? How do you think

I've lasted out here alone all these years without you?
I'm just as capable as you."

She leaned on the sink breathing hard.

"Are you done?" I said.

She didn't answer.

"Look, the reason I didn't think about you is
because I'm not looking for an equal, I'm looking for
a patsy. Someone to send out first so I don't get
killed. That's not you. You're very capable. That's
why I have more respect than to ask you to be a
sidekick."

"Sidekick?"

"That's what I'm looking for."

Her breathing returned to normal, and she shot me
a sideways look.

"I guess that's not so bad," she said.

"I'd like you to be my backup," I said. "Much
more important than a sidekick."

I reached into my pocket and pulled out the
prepaid cell phone.

"Do you know how to work one of these?"

She looked at the phone.

"I'm old," she said. "Not stupid."

I grinned.

"So, you'll do it?" I said. "Be my backup?"

She stared at the phone for a long moment.

"This doesn't mean we're going steady or anything," I said.

She smiled.

"You're such an idiot," she said taking the phone. "Yes. I'll be your backup."

"Sweet!"

"So, I go like this?" she said holding the phone up to her ear without opening it.

A look of panic crossed my face. She held the phone against her head for a long moment before smiling. She flipped it open and pressed the power key.

"Oh," I said, feeling the panic drain away. "I'm the idiot?"

She laughed, smacked me in the shoulder, and pushed me through the door.

"Get out of here and go find your sidekick," she said.

I rubbed my sore shoulder on the way out.

I drove to the station and told Dell I was taking a leave of absence. He grunted acknowledgement and I drove to town to find Billy.

I pulled into the diner that sat on the edge of town, went in, and grabbed a seat. The booth made that scrunching sound when I plopped down in it and I could feel my pants sticking to it. I picked up the laminated menu that had something on it that looked like dried blood. I hoped it was old gravy and perused the choices.

When you've sat on the deck of a yacht in the middle of the Mediterranean eating caviar it's kinda tough to go back to eating at a greasy spoon. Looking at the silverware they seemed to take that title seriously. There were what I hoped were water spots on the cutlery.

Billy walked up with a pad and pen in hand.

"How are you?" he said with a grin.

"Doing good," I said. "How about you?"

"You know," he said. "Living the dream."

"I see. How would you like a job?"

"I already have two, thanks."

"I can pay you more than both," I said. "How does a thousand dollars a week sound?"

He ripped off his apron.

"Sounds like you've got yourself an employee."

"Don't you even want to know what you'd be doing?"

"For a grand a week, I don't care."

"Alright then," I said. "Your first job is to put the apron back on and go make me a BLT."

"What?"

"You have to at least tell your boss you're quitting, and I'm hungry," I said. "Go make me a sammich."

He looked at me questioningly as he slowly put the apron back on and walked away.

Twenty minutes later he returned with the sandwich.

I grabbed it and took a big bite.

"You tell your boss you're quitting?" I said, spraying lettuce and bits of bread all over the table.

"Not yet," he said. "I figured I'd wait until the end of my shift."

I nodded and took another big bite as he walked off to take care of other customers.

I finished my lunch, paid, and went to the truck. When his shift was over, I saw him talk to the manager who didn't seem very happy, and then walk out.

"When do I start?" he said stepping out to the truck.

"Right now, get in."

His jaw dropped and he looked like he wanted to ask a question, but he silently went around to the other side and got in the truck.

I went to the store and bought some supplies, then to the realtor, then out to the property I'd just bought. It was an old ranch that was on the opposite side of town from the park.

I parked the truck halfway down the driveway, surrounded by a field, got out, and nailed a target to a tree.

"Ok," I said. "First lesson, do you know how to shoot a gun?"

He pashawed me and said, "Of course."

I handed him the tranquilizer gun and pointed at the target hanging ten feet away.

"Fire away," I said.

He took the gun and held it by the barrel, then looked inside.

I grabbed it from him.

"Ok, so you don't know how to shoot a gun."

He hung his head.

"No."

"And you've lived out here in the country for how long?"

"All my life."

"Alright, rule number one, don't lie to me," I said. "If you don't know something, tell me. We'll figure it out."

He nodded.

"Ok, here's how you hold the gun," I said showing him. "This is how you load it. Here is where the safety is. And most of all, this is the barrel. Don't ever point this at me."

We practiced for a while. Loading, unloading, aiming, before he ever pulled the trigger. Once we started shooting, it turned out he wasn't a bad shot. After getting used to the tranq gun I gave him something a little more powerful, my .45. It took him a little while to get used to the new dynamics. With his first shot he almost let the gun hit him in the forehead. We practiced grips and recoil control after that.

"Is all this training really necessary to be a park ranger?" he said.

"No, but it is for what we'll be doing."

"What's that?"

"Our goal is to bring unique creatures in alive and unharmed, if possible," I said. "The .45 is only a last resort weapon when everything else has failed and something is eating my face off."

"Has that ever happened?" he said.

I looked at him, dumbfounded.

"Yeah, kid," I said, sarcastically. "This is the third time I've had reconstructive surgery."

He stared at my face in awe.

"They did a really good job."

I shook my head starting to rethink this whole sidekick thing.

"What creatures?" he said.

"Cryptids."

He stared at me blankly.

I sighed.

"You know, Bigfoot, Jersey Devil, Siren, Banshee, pretty much any creature that's outside the normal conventions."

"Wow, I never realized those were real."

"Ok, moving on," I said. "Do you know how to drive?"

"Of course I… "

I glared at him.

"No," he said, lowering his head. "After I failed my driver's test the fifth time, my parents told me no more."

"That seems a bit harsh," I said tossing him the keys. "It couldn't be that bad."

Twenty minutes later as I sat in the passenger seat, fighting my way out of the giant marshmallow of death, smoke rolled from under the crumpled hood. I turned to him.

"We're in an open field," I said slowly. "There was literally one tree in the entire area, and you managed to hit it."

"Sorry," he said looking like a whipped puppy.

I held out my hand.

"Give me those keys," I said.

He pulled them out of the ignition and handed them to me. I threw them as far as I could into the field.

"Bad Tommy," I said, lightly smacking his fingers.

"My name's Billy," he said, looking at his offended digits.

"Whatever," I said. "Let's go."

"Where?"

"Without a truck, we're walking to town."

He shrugged and started walking beside me.

"What kind of shape are you in?" I said.

"I can hold my own."

"Oh really," I said. "Then run to town and run back to me while I walk."

He looked across the field to the town in the distance.

"Why?" he said.

"First of all, because I want to see what kind of shape you're in, second because I said so, and third... " I turned and pointed at the pillar of smoke that was rising from the truck.

He sighed and started jogging.

"Run, Forrest!" I yelled, causing him to stop and put his hands on his hips.

"That's not funny," he said.

I pulled out my wallet.

"I'll tell you what," I said. "If you can make it to town, get me a soda from the machine in front of the hardware store, and be back in twenty minutes, I'll give you a thousand-dollar bonus right here."

He disappeared in a cloud of dust.

I set the timer on my watch and kept walking at a leisurely pace.

Nineteen minutes later an exhausted Billy trudged up to me holding a soda.

"Great job, Tommy," I said looking at my watch.

"B... Billy," he said as he collapsed on the ground.

He panted as he lay out flat, arms and legs spread, looking every bit like he was about to make a snow angel in the field.

I sat beside him and enjoyed my soda.

"It's kinda warm," I said holding up the can.

He turned his head to look at me.

"Next time I'll strap the machine to my back, your majesty," he said.

I smiled inwardly. It was good to know he would stand up to me if needed. But I wasn't going to let him know that.

"Well, that comment just cost you a hundred dollars," I said sipping my soda.

"What? Just for being sarcastic?"

"Who's the boss?" I said.

"You are."

"Did you back-talk your boss at the store?"

"Hell no, he'd have me in a headlock before I could say boo."

"Then why should you back-talk me?"

He thought for a long moment. I could see there were a few more comments he wanted to say, but in the end, he kept his mouth shut.

"Are you done with your break?" I said finishing my soda and tossing the can in the field.

"Are you serious?" he said. "I just ran over a mile and back."

"Ok," I said getting up. "Catch up when you're ready."

I pulled out my wallet and tossed nine brand new hundred-dollar bills on the ground beside him, then continued walking toward town.

Around ten minutes later he caught up with me and we walked in silence the rest of the way.

When we reached the edge of town, he started toward the right, and I went left.

"Aren't we going to the car dealership?" he said pointing down the street.

"I'm hungry," I said. "Walking to town after someone destroyed my truck has given me an appetite."

He hung his head and followed me into the local diner. The boss was shooting him dirty looks the whole time. I wondered if there would be 'special sauce' on my food as well as his.

We walked out an hour later with full bellies and went to the car dealership. I bought three trucks, got in one, and had the other two delivered.

"Why three?" Billy said as he fastened his seatbelt.

"In case I lose my mind and let you drive again."

"So, you bought a spare truck like I would buy a spare pack of gum?"

I shrugged. "I guess."

"I guess this creature, cryptid hunting thing pays pretty well."

"Yep."

"So, we have to be careful catching these things even though they're trying to kill us?"

"Pretty much," I said. "You still want the job?"

"Absolutely," he said. "I love those little 's's with the lines through them."

"Ah, a humanitarian."

"A what?"

"Never mind."

"So, the park ranger thing is just for a cover story, right."

"That's the plan."

"I'm just not sure how many people are gonna fall for that."

I pulled over and looked at him.

"Do you always talk this much?"

"I guess."

"Let's dial that back a bit, shall we?"

"What?"

"Don't talk so much," I said rolling my eyes. "And if I hold my finger up to my lips like this, don't talk at all."

"But what if… ?"

I held my finger up to my lips and he stopped talking.

We drove to the ranger station.

"Stay," I said, pointing at him as I walked into the station.

"Where have you been?" Sharon said. "Dell has been beside himself and the rest of us have to make up for your work."

The entire time she was talking I was walking straight towards Dell's office. When I got there, she stepped in front of the door.

"We were told you weren't allowed in here," she said.

I smiled, grabbed her shoulders, and slid her from in front of the door. I tried the knob, and it was locked.

"See?" she said folding her arms in front of her chest.

I looked around and found an ashtray, threw it through the window, then reached through and unlocked the door.

"What the hell?" she said. "I'm calling Dell."

I reached into my pocket and pulled out a wad of cash.

She put down the phone.

"As soon as I see something that Dell needs to know about because I don't see anything happening right now."

She grabbed the cash, and I pointed toward the front door. She got the hint and left.

I dug through Dell's files, not finding what I wanted, then broke into his locked file drawer and hit paydirt. I took the thick file with me that read, 'Cryptids'.

I walked out the front door and said to Sharon without looking at her, "I'm done, you can go back in now. I was never here."

I got in the truck and drove to my new home.

"Come on in, kid," I said hopping out of the truck and opening the front door.

He cringed looking at the house.

"Do I have to?" he said.

"Why? What's wrong?"

"Are you seriously looking at this old house that screams, 'haunted' and asking me what's wrong?"

"It's just an old house," I said. "Come on."

"I've seen this house somewhere before," Billy said as he got out of the truck and paused. He looked over the old house that was more like a mansion, and then it hit him. He ran up to the door and peeked inside.

"I know where I've seen this place from," he said.

"Oh, yeah?" I said, pulling tarps off furniture and sending clouds of dust into the air and myself into a coughing fit. "Where?"

"You ever play the Resident Evil remake they did for the Gamecube?"

"What's a Gamecube?" I said. "Is that like a Rubik's Cube?"

He rolled his eyes at me.

"I can't believe you don't know the Gamecube is a video game system."

"Sorry, kid," I said pulling off another tarp. "Some of us live in the real world."

"And fight Cryptids for a living?"

"Ouch!" I said. "Good comeback. That'll cost you a hundred off this week's salary."

"Is there anything I can say without getting my salary docked?"

I thought about it for a moment.

"If you say yes, you shouldn't get your salary docked."

"Should I use my first paycheck to buy me a dog collar?" he whispered under his breath.

I turned away and smiled, pretending not to hear him.

"So, what about this video game?" I said.

"Oh, yeah, It's about this mansion that I swear looks exactly like this."

"Ok, and?"

"And it was full of zombies and traps and freaky keys to unlock different doors."

"Zombies, you say?" I said looking around. "I don't think that's on my list, but maybe in the basement. Go check."

"You want me to check the basement?" he said as if I'd just asked him to swim across a lake of fire.

"Yep."

"Alone?"

"Unless you have a mouse in your pocket."

He looked at the basement door.

"Do I have to?"

"What's the word that doesn't get your salary docked?"

He hung his head.

"Yes."

"Ok then, get to it."

I continued removing tarps from the furniture. The antiques in the house were in pristine condition. Even the couches and chairs looked like they hadn't been sat on for years.

I whipped off another tarp and discovered a grandfather clock. It was perfect except for a few scratches on the side where the door was opened to wind it.

As I was admiring it, I heard a shout from the basement. I ran to the door and dashed down the stairs, gun in hand, looking around for where the attack was coming from.

I found Billy standing in a corner of a much larger-than-expected basement. I ran over to him.

"What's wrong?" I said breathless.

"Look," he said pointing at a metal utility shelf.

I looked for whatever else there was to look at, but there was nothing. The shelf had a few old paint cans and various junk on it.

"It's a shelf," I said.

He smiled and slid the rusty paint can to the side.

A five-foot section of concrete wall swung open revealing a dark hallway.

We looked at each other with genuine excitement.

"Got any flashlights?" he said.

I ran out to the truck, grabbed two flashlights then ran back inside. When I got to the wall, the door was closed, and Billy was gone.

I slid the paint can and the door swung open to reveal Billy standing just inside the hallway, shaking.

I handed him a flashlight.

"You ok?" I said.

"I couldn't find the way to open it back up."

"How about this? I'll go in and look for the trigger to open the door from the inside and you wait here in case I need you to trigger it from out here."

He nodded silently.

I stepped into the hallway and began searching for something that looked like a trigger. It took a minute to decide that the metal torch holder had scrape marks at the bottom of it. I slid it to the side and the door swung open almost hitting Billy.

"I found it," I said showing him the torch holder.

"Ok," he said softly. It seemed like his excitement had drained away.

I started down the hallway and Billy followed along behind. He jumped when the door swung closed. We shone our lights ahead, looking for anything, especially lights. We walked for several minutes before coming to another door. I looked at him and he seemed terrified to see what was behind it.

I opened it and was surprised to see daylight. I walked outside and turned to look at the outside of the door only to find it was a tree, or at least it looked like the outside of a tree. I was astounded to find we were a hundred yards or more away from the house.

"That's cool," I said.

"Yeah," he said without enthusiasm.

"We can walk back to the house from here. We don't have to use the creepy dark tunnel."

He sighed deeply.

"Thanks."

We started walking and for the first time, I was worried about this kid and how he was going to do against his first cryptid.

'Do I really want to do this to him?' I thought.

Chapter 6

It was late evening when the pounding started. Billy and I were finishing up our walk through the house, deciding which room would be the office.

When I got down to the door, I could see dust falling from the doorframe. The assault continued non-stop until I opened the door and there stood Dell.

"What's up?" I said.

"You know exactly what's up!" he screamed. "How dare you break into my office and steal my files."

"Ok, you know what, I'm not listening to this," I said, pushing the door closed.

He jammed his shoulder into it and flung it back open.

"Don't even think you're getting away with this," he said stomping into the room.

"I should let you know that you're trespassing right now and I'm fully within my rights to do whatever's necessary should I feel my life is in danger."

"You're threatening me now? I'm sure the sheriff would like to hear about that."

"Why? Is he in on your little coverup?"

"What coverup?"

"I read the file. I know what's out there. My only question is why the secrecy?"

"You have no idea what you're talking about," he said still advancing on me.

I put my hands on his chest and shoved him back.

"Enough!" I said. "I won't be harassed or bullied in my own house."

"You assaulted me," he said with a grin. "Your word against mine."

"What's going on?" Billy said from the top of the stairs.

I turned to him and grinned.

"You were saying?"

"He's just a kid," Dell said frowning. "No one will believe him anyway."

"Tommy… " I said.

"Billy."

"Whatever, will you go get my gun please?" I said staring Dell in the eyes. "Mr. Stanton was just leaving."

Billy disappeared down the hallway and came right back holding my .45 by the barrel. I cringed as he ran down the stairs holding it so that the barrel was pointed right at him. I grabbed it away from him as soon as he reached the bottom.

"Thanks, Tommy," I said.

"Billy."

"Whatever."

I turned to point the gun at Dell, but he wasn't there. Instead, there was a quivering ball of fur that was growing larger by the second. I looked out the window and the light from the newly risen moon was shining in. I stared at it for a moment and realized it was full.

"Uh oh," I said mesmerized by the expanding fur on Dell's increasingly muscular arms.

Billy's mouth hung wide open, and his eyes were big as saucers as he watched Dell complete his transformation.

I emptied the clip into his chest as he stood and towered over me. The gun firing was deafening in the foyer of the house. Billy had covered his ears but was still watching as the bullets seemed to have no effect on this creature whatsoever.

I stared at the gun, then at Dell.

"So, this would be the part where I apologize for any offense I may have inadvertently caused," I said to Dell as he stood growling at me. "This new development changes our relationship drastically and I would like to pledge that I will be an exemplary employee from this moment on. I'd also like to add that I would be more than willing to forget this whole incident and make a sizable donation to your personal retirement fund. Shall we say a million dollars?"

His red eyes glared down at me, and he unleashed a deafening roar that was somehow louder than the gunfire.

"I'll take that as a no," I said, then turned to Billy and said, "Run!"

He stood there transfixed. There was a dark stain on the front of his jeans running down his leg. I ran toward him and tackled him into a running fireman's carry up the stairs, two at a time. I dove into the first door and locked it, collapsing against it.

"That... was... a... " Billy said, stammering.

"Yes," I said, breathing hard. "My boss is a little upset with me at the moment. But I think if we give him a little time to cool down, things will be fine."

I was hoping to get a respite when a set of claws ripped through the door.

"Or not," I said jumping up and looking for anything to use for a weapon.

"Where's your cell phone?" I said as I searched.

"I don't have a cell phone," he said as the door continued to disintegrate under the assault.

"What? I thought every kid had a cell phone."

"Not ones who can't afford it."

"Ok, tomorrow I'm buying you a cell phone," I said looking at the door that was nearly gone.

"If we live that long," he said.

The door exploded inward, and Dell burst into the room looking around.

"Tommy… "

"Billy."

"Whatever, go stand in the corner," I said as Dell stalked toward me.

"What did I do wrong?"

"Nothing, just go stand in the corner."

He stepped over to the corner as I backed away towards the wall. Dell glanced at him but kept his focus on me. I kept backing until I had nowhere to go. I looked behind me and saw curtains. Fear flooded my eyes as I slid along the wall looking for any place to go.

Dell crouched, loading his legs for the killing lunge.

I waited for death to take me. Once again, I doubted my continued risking of life and limb when I had more money than I could possibly spend. I glanced at Billy thinking that my sidekick taking the fall idea hadn't panned out either. It seemed like Dolores was right. One day my luck was going to run out.

Today looked like that day.

Dell sprung.

I lunged to the right with every ounce of strength in me.

He tried to change his direction in midair, but inertia told him it didn't work that way. His powerful legs had launched him on a straight path towards me. Now his path was straight towards a window.

The glass shattered and the drapes parted like the cape of a bullfighter, leaving Dell grasping at air as he sailed out into the night.

I lay on my stomach and turned back toward the window to see my handiwork.

"You did it!" Billy said.

"Did what?" I said crawling to my feet. "Do you really think he's going to tuck his tail between his legs and slink off like a whipped puppy? He'll be back as soon as his feet hit the ground?"

Terror washed over his face.

"What do we do?"

"I need my phone," I said, heading downstairs. "Do you remember where I set it?"

"I thought you had it in your pocket."

I patted myself down just to double-check.

"Nope, I remember setting it down somewhere."

"Is a phone really the most important thing right now?" he said.

"More than you can imagine," I said as we reached the ground floor and headed toward the kitchen.

I searched around on the counter and anywhere else I could, but it wasn't there. As an afterthought, I grabbed the biggest butcher knife I could find.

"Bullets didn't hurt him," Billy said. "What good will that do?"

I looked at the knife and then at Billy.

"At least I won't die for lack of trying."

He looked at the knife, then me, and grabbed the next biggest knife in the drawer.

"So, what's the plan?" he said.

"Don't die."

"I like that plan."

Just then we heard a crash coming from the foyer announcing that Dell was back in the house.

I put my finger up to my lips and snuck over to the basement door. I opened it and ushered him inside, then closed it as quietly as possible.

We went down the staircase slowly and carefully.

"Do you still have your flashlight?" I whispered.

He nodded as we continued to sneak down the stairs. I could hear the floorboards creak as Dell stalked around upstairs searching for us. He was walking slowly. I was sure he was listening for any sound.

We were almost to the bottom when one of the stairs creaked.

I froze.

The footsteps upstairs stopped.

I motioned for Billy to be still.

For the longest time, no one moved.

I tried not to breathe.

Billy held his breath.

You know how in the movies the one being chased makes a noise and the predator comes toward him only to have him throw a rock in another direction and the predator chases off after it.

I wished I could do that right now. And then I realized something. I reached into my pocket and pulled out a set of truck keys. I pressed the panic button on the remote and heard the horn honking repeatedly.

The footsteps upstairs ran towards the sound.

I took a breath.

"Let's go," I whispered to Billy as we continued the rest of the way down the stairs and over to the secret passage.

We opened the door and closed it behind us.

I slid to the floor and sat feeling more exhausted than I had in a long time.

"Now what?" Billy said.

"I don't know."

"You don't know?"

"No, I don't know."

"How can you not know?" he said. "I thought you'd been doing this cryptid hunting thing for a while."

"That doesn't mean I have it all figured out," I growled. "I just kinda go with the situation."

"Seems pretty dangerous to deal with these things without having a plan."

"Alright, smart guy," I snapped. "What's your big plan?"

He thought for a moment.

"We could wait him out."

"Like wait for him to catch a bus out of town?" I said sarcastically.

"No, I mean he's a werewolf, right? So, we wait for the moon to go down or the sun to come up and he changes back to a human."

I looked at my watch. It was eleven fifteen at night.

"Nine hours of waiting?" I said.

"It beats dying."

I shook my head.

"No, I need my phone," I said. "I get my phone, make a call and ten minutes later this is all over."

"Ok, so where did you have it last?"

"I've been trying to remember," I said. "But I've been a little busy with my homicidal, supernatural boss trying to relocate my head to somewhere other than my body."

"I've got it!" he said snapping his fingers.

"Is it contagious?" I said scooting away from him.

"What? No, I mean I know where your phone is."

"Where?"

"In your truck," he said. "Remember you left it there to charge?"

I sighed.

"You mean the truck that Dell's currently tearing limb from limb?"

"Oh," he said, his face going from triumph to defeat. "Yeah, that truck."

I stood and started walking to the far end of the hallway.

"Where are we going?" he said, following along.

"I need that phone," I said.

He glanced from me to the door we had just entered.

"Why not go that way?"

"Because once Dell is done dismembering my truck, he'll come back in the house looking for us," I said. "I'm hoping that we can sneak around and get that phone while he's busy trying to find and kill us."

"Yeah," he said without enthusiasm. "Great plan."

"Do I need to dock you another hundred?" I said.

He shook his head and made the zip the lip and throw away the key motion.

I turned away and grinned. I was going to like working with this kid if we lived long enough.

***

We reached the end of the hallway having not spoken the entire time. I realized that it was the longest he'd gone without talking, at least around me.

"Ok, here's the deal," I said. "I have no idea where he's going to be. For all I know he's waiting outside this door to grab us."

Billy stared at the door as if it had just morphed into a demon.

I snapped my fingers in front of his eyes.

"Focus," I said. "We need to get to my truck and find that phone. If we get split up and you get to the phone first, dial the number on the top of the list and tell The Man that I have an emergency and I need him here for assistance right now. Tell him it's more urgent than Mrs. Foot."

"What?"

"Don't worry, he'll understand."

"Why am I doing this?" he said. "Where will you be?"

"I figured I'd run to town and get a pedicure while we wait for Dell to go away."

"I didn't think any shops were open this late."

I smacked my forehead with my palm.

"It's just in case you get to the phone first or I get tied up running for my life."

"Oh, ok."

I eyed him doubtfully.

"Are we clear?"

"Yep."

I wasn't filled with confidence but opened the door anyway.

We snuck out and closed the door then turned back to look at the house. The lights were on, but I couldn't see any movement. The truck alarm was no longer going off. I was going to have to make some kind of deal with the local car dealership if I was going to continue destroying vehicles at this rate.

I made him turn off the flashlight as we snuck back towards the house. There was no need to announce our presence and the full moon gave off enough light for us to see our way. It filled the field with an ominous eerie glow. Ironically, the same moon that initiated our problem was now assisting us.

I stopped when we heard a long mournful wail in the distance.

"What's that?" he whispered.

I knew exactly what it was. It was Dolores doing her job and announcing someone's death. I really hoped it wasn't ours, but since I could hear it, I knew the unfortunate truth.

"It sounds like a fox," I said as we kept moving towards the house.

The closer we got the more I could feel eyes on me. The house was lit up and very inviting if I didn't know death was lurking inside.

We got to the edge of the house and snuck around the side toward the front. At each window, we got down on our hands and knees to crawl underneath in hopes of avoiding being spotted.

When we came to the front corner of the house, I paused and took a long slow look at any place he could be hiding.

My truck was smashed of course and laying on its roof. It seemed like Godzilla had used it for soccer practice.

"Now what?" Billy whispered in my ear making me jump.

"Now all I have to do is get to the truck, find my phone that could be literally anywhere, hope that it still works, call the man to come and help us, then wait ten minutes and pray that my boss, who already hates me and has now turned into a giant superhuman schnauzer on steroids, doesn't see, hear, or smell us and turn us into little piles of pâté."

"What's pâté?"

I shook my head. "I'll tell you later," I whispered.

I took a step toward the truck and heard him follow behind me.

"No," I whispered. "Stay here."

"But I... "

"No. Stay," I said, pointing at the ground. "Sit. Stay."

He opened his mouth but I raised my finger and he remained silent and sat down.

"Good boy," I whispered patting him on the head.

I took another look around then snuck over to the truck, staying low, moving as quickly and quietly as I could. I went to the side that was away from the house, so I would at least be in shadow and out of direct view… mostly.

The cab was nearly collapsed. I pulled out the flashlight and covered it with my hand allowing a tiny sliver of light to peek through my fingers. I used the minuscule ray of light to search through the detritus of the cab. Fortunately, I hadn't had the truck long enough to accumulate the insane amounts of trash and lost items that gathered under the seats of most vehicles.

It took a few minutes of looking. I had to crawl inside to search the driver's side, which meant I had to crawl over glass, lots of glass. Until I reached the driver's side, my palms and elbows were damp with blood.

I did my best to ignore the pain and focus on the goal of finding that little life-saving piece of metal and plastic. I didn't find it on the ceiling (floor?) so I turned my gaze upwards. Surprisingly, it was lodged in the door handle. I had to jiggle it loose and it slipped out of my bloody hands, falling to the floor (ceiling?)

I grabbed it and didn't wait to get out of the truck. I pressed the power button.

Nothing.

I silently cursed when I noticed the back wasn't on tightly. I snapped it together and then pressed the power button again.

For the ten longest seconds of my life, nothing happened. And then the logo lit up.

I nearly shouted, until I remembered what a huge mistake that would've been.

The phone came to full power and booted up. I covered the speaker when the little 'tah-dah' noise sounded. Then I pulled up my contacts and dialed The Man Who Doesn't Exist.

It rang eight times before I heard a click.

"You need to get here now... " I said as an electronic voice talked over me.

"We're sorry, the number you have reached has a voice mailbox that hasn't been set up. Goodbye."

I stared in horror at the phone as the line went dead, just like I was about to.

I dialed again and got the same message.

I dialed five more times and got the same results. Einstein would've loved me right then.

I stared at the phone as if it was the one who had betrayed me, then I remembered and called the other number.

"Hello?" Dolores said on the second ring.

"I'm in trouble. I need backup."

"I know, I'm on my way."

"How did you… ? Never mind, when will you be here?"

"I'm not sure," she said. "Could be ten minutes, maybe less."

"For my sake and the kid's sake, I hope it's less."

I hung up and breathed a partial sigh of relief. At least someone cared enough to come to my… to *our* rescue.

I peered over at the house in the dead of night, with random lights turned on, it did look a little spooky. I got a chill that had nothing to do with the temperature when I saw Dell emerge from the destroyed front door. He glanced around the yard and his gaze settled on the truck.

I stayed frozen to the spot, not daring to move a millimeter. His eyes seemed to narrow on the truck as if he saw me. For a long moment, he stared right into my eyes. I moved my thumb just enough to make sure the flashlight was off. If he was going to find me, he would have to do it without any help from me.

Suddenly, he turned and started walking along the porch toward the side of the house where Billy sat waiting.

I peered over and Billy was sitting there leaning against the house, oblivious to the danger approaching him.

I crawled as quickly as I could backward out of the truck, shredding my hands and elbows even more. By the time I was free, Dell was nearly to the end of the porch.

I duck-walked to the front of the truck and waved frantically at Billy. He spotted me and waved back. I waved in a push-away motion, trying to get him to run away. He shrugged at me and held up his hands showing he didn't understand.

I tried to imitate running without standing up and giving away my position, but it was a massive failure. Not only did he not understand, but Dell had seen him making motions and moved in for the kill.

I had only one decision to make. I stood up and yelled at the top of my lungs, "RUN!"

Dell glared at me.

Billy glanced at Dell.

I stared at Billy.

Dell paused for a moment and saw me staring at Billy who was frozen in terror and hadn't moved except to start shaking.

I saw the look on Dell's face as he saw me watching Billy. I don't know if werewolves can smile or not, but I swear this one did as he lunged at Billy and began tearing him to shreds.

"NO!" I screamed as I ran straight at him, in opposition to every survival instinct.

I pulled the knife out of my pocket and leaped onto his back, slashing at him with the ferocity of a cornered animal.

He roared in pain as the knife tore into his back. The blade seemed to take on a life of its own, stabbing repeatedly, faster than I thought possible.

He rolled forward, flipping me off his back and following where I landed. I rolled and came up holding the knife in front of me as he charged. I slashed at his throat, just missing but hitting his shoulder.

He roared again as he planted his feet for another attack. This time I fell flat on my back as he flew over top of me so close, I could feel his hot breath on my face. I kicked straight up as he passed over, nailing him exactly where I wanted to.

He got up a little more slowly the next time and held his paws between his legs. I quickly stood and held the knife at the ready.

He got down on all fours and ran at me with blinding speed as I prepared to jump over him. But he had anticipated my move and leaped at the last moment, catching me in the midsection and tackling me to the ground.

He landed on top of me and snapped at my face with his jaws of death. The only thing that kept him from chewing right through my face was the knife I held against his throat. The blade dug in deeper the more he tried to move his head back and forth to get a bite on me. For the briefest of moments, I wondered if he would literally saw his own head off just to get to me.

But while his head was occupied, his arms weren't. His razor-sharp claws slashed at my arms and sides grinding them to hamburger. There was no way around it, I was in a losing battle. It was only a matter of how long I prolonged the inevitable.

In my final moments, my only regret was I didn't care enough about anyone to wish I had said goodbye.

…

The scream pierced my ears like an icepick.

At first, I thought Dell was screaming as a victory cry over my dead body. But then the crushing weight lifted off me. I opened my eyes to see Dell holding his ears and howling in pain.

With enormous effort, I rolled my head to the side toward the sound and saw Dolores screaming at Dell. He was stumbling backward at the audible assault. Dolores walked steadily toward him, unleashing her scream as she went.

As if being bombarded, Dell began swiping back and forth with his claws as though fighting off the sound. Finally, he succumbed and fell to his knees.

Blinding light came from everywhere.

Soldiers grabbed Dell with a net. He struggled against it, but there were many tasers built into it and one shock was all he needed to go limp and be carried off.

Dolores came over and knelt beside me.

"Are you alright?" she said.

"Oh yeah, I'm super," I said trying to get up and falling back to the ground. "I just need a minute. Go check on the kid."

She glanced over and saw the medic working on him.

"They're already looking after him," she said helping me up to a sitting position.

"Don't stain your dress," I said as she held my bloody arm.

She smiled. "I know how to get blood stains out."

"I'm sure you do," I said getting painfully to my feet.

The Man Who Doesn't Exist came toward me but stopped when he saw Dolores.

He nodded to her.

"Dolores," he said stiffly.

"Thomas," she said back.

He stepped closer to me and held out his hand.

"Sorry I… "

That's as far as he got before I belted him across the chin, nearly falling in the process.

He stumbled then straightened himself and rubbed his jaw. Four soldiers started toward me, but the man held up his hand and they stopped.

"Where were you?" I yelled. "I called because I needed help right away. But you didn't answer."

"You're right," he said. "I didn't."

"That's it? I didn't? Nothing else, like what was more important than my life?"

"I do apologize," he said. "However, it's difficult to predict when you'll need help."

"Well, yeah, it's difficult to know when my pissed-off boss is gonna show up at my front door and then suddenly turn into a giant Poodle on steroids," I said. "Did you know?"

"Know what?"

"Know what Dell was?"

He nodded.

"Don't you think that was information I needed?" I said getting in his face.

He shrugged.

"You didn't need me to tell you there was a Bigfoot out there, or a Jersey Devil, or a Chupacabra, or a Siren," he considered Dolores. "Or a Banshee. You've handled them one by one. I didn't think I needed to tell you about one that might never come after you."

"Even when I see him almost every day?"

"Maybe you shouldn't piss off your boss," he said with a sharp look.

"Maybe my boss should answer his damn phone when I call, instead of throwing vague threats at me."

"Who said it was vague?" he said glowering at me.

"Both of you need to stop," Dolores said. "He showed up," she told me. "It may have been a little late but he's here."

"As always," The Man said.

"And you," Dolores turned toward him. "If one of your men didn't answer your call, you'd be livid, wouldn't you?"

"I don't know about livid… " he said.

"I know you would," she said. "You might even give him his walking papers."

The Man opened his mouth then closed it at a look from her.

"The question is can I depend on you?" I said to the man.

"You can."

"How much? Ninety percent of the time? Eighty?"

"I know it's difficult, but you must understand… "

"No, all I have to understand is that I needed you and you weren't there."

"We're here now."

"Tell that to Tommy," I said pointing over to where the medic was working on him.

I heard a weak voice say, "Billy."

I hobbled over and saw a pair of eyes looking up from what seemed like a slab of raw meat. There were claw marks across his right eye, but the eye itself seemed to be intact. The rest of him was covered in blood. I stumbled and Dolores caught me and held me up with more strength than I would've thought she possessed.

"We need to get him to a hospital now," the medic said looking back and forth from me to the man.

"Was he bitten?" the man asked.

"What does that matter?" I said. "He needs a hospital."

"It could matter a great deal," he said.

"Would you just get him to a hospital and quit being so... you?" I said, glaring at him.

He held my gaze for a moment then sighed and said, "Let's get him to the hospital."

The medic and a couple of soldiers got him on a backboard and into the helicopter. The man stepped in as well and stared straight ahead.

"And when he's able, bring him back here, not to your little zoo," I said.

"You might regret that," he said.

"I might regret a lot of things I've said and done tonight," I said looking at him. "But I doubt it."

"What about you?" he said. "Don't you want to go to the hospital?"

I eyed Dolores and she nodded.

"I think we'll manage," I said.

"Are you sure?"

"Dolores was here to help when you weren't," I said. "I think we can do ok without you."

Then I turned my back on him and started walking away with Dolores steadying me.

I didn't look when I heard the helicopter take off.

I kept walking until it was out of sight, then stopped and turned toward Dolores.

"You don't drive, do you?"

"No."

I sighed and then searched for the number of the only taxi service in town.

Half an hour later we walked into the emergency room.

Chapter 7

You'd think by now I would've gotten used to hospitals. The incessant sounds of the machines, the God-awful disinfectant smell they use to cover the stench of death, the artificially cheerful nurses who obviously can't stand you, and the astronomical prices they charge for everything.

But no. I still hate hospitals, just in case you couldn't tell.

I lay in the uncomfortable bed and stared at the white wall. I had lost track of how long I'd been here. I refused to plug in my phone, and it had since gone dead. I really didn't feel like talking to anyone anyway. I especially didn't want to hear from The Man Who Doesn't Exist. I needed to come up with a better name for him. I could think of several right now, but that was just because I was still mad.

Wait, that's not right. I'm not mad, I'm furious, livid, indignant, incensed, outraged, enraged (are those the same thing?) Anyway, I'm miffed. And I didn't want to hear any halfhearted apologies. Or even worse, I didn't want to hear him try to gloss over the fact that he failed, and it nearly cost me my life.

I had no idea how the kid was doing and that made me even madder. One phone call would've been nice. But no, I didn't want to talk to him. The man, not Billy.

I was so mad I was confusing myself.

I needed to calm down. And nothing calms me down more than spending some of my hard-earned money.

I plugged in my phone and waited for the battery to charge a little, then started making phone calls. I ignored the messages as long as I could. I called contractors, vendors, and merchants. I hired a project manager and gave her precise instructions.

After a few hours of spending money, I started to feel better. Maybe even good enough to look at some messages.

I checked the texts and they were all from the medic, all but one. She said the man knew I wouldn't want to talk to him, so he told her to give me status updates on the kid.

He'd made it through surgery and was in critical but stable condition.

I read the text from The Man. It was right to the point.

'Money delivered, usual amount.'

That was it.

I wasn't sure what I was expecting or even what I wanted. I knew he wasn't going to beg and plead for forgiveness. I wasn't even sure what I felt about the whole thing. Was it anger that he didn't bail me out yet again? Was it bruised ego that he didn't answer my call like I wasn't important enough? Or was it just plain fear at the reminder that one of these days he won't get there in time and that'll be game over?

I started to text back, then deleted the message and closed the phone.

Aside from not knowing what to say, I figured it would drive him nuts that I had started typing, then never sent the message.

I laid in bed and focused on being in pain, just like the other times I've been in the hospital over the last few months. I wondered how much more my body could take.

I stared at my arms which were completely covered in bandages all the way down to my palms. Fortunately, I was able to bend at the joints.

I opened the phone and texted the medic, 'Where's Tommy?'

'You mean Billy?' came the response.

'Whatever, where is he?'

'Two floors above you in critical care.'

'Is he allowed visitors?'

'As if you care what's allowed.'

'No need to be sassy,' I texted.

'Yes, he's allowed visitors. I've been by to see him a couple of times.'

'Well, aren't you sweet?'

'Just shut up and go see him.'

'Yes, sir!'

'Darn right.'

I smiled as I closed the phone and pressed the nurse call button.

"Can I help you?" came a voice that managed to sound bored and busy at the same time.

"Can you bring me a wheelchair?"

"What for?"

"I want to go see a friend."

"I'm too busy for such nonsense."

"Ok," I said then used an app to find the hospital administrator's number.

After a short conversation about how I was an investor and was tempted to buy the hospital, a wheelchair suddenly appeared in my room along with a disgruntled nurse.

"Anything else, Your Majesty?" she said.

"A push up to critical care," I said.

"I'm way too busy to drive you around like some hospital Uber."

"That's fine," I said picking up my phone.

"Who are you calling?"

"The administrator," I said humming lazily. "I sure hope you have your resume updated."

She nearly fell over the wheelchair dragging it over to my bed and getting me into it.

"Hello?" the administrator said on the phone.

"Hello, again, I just wanted to tell you that I've got nurse… " I glanced at her nametag. "Cheryl here and she's being super helpful."

"That's great!" he said. "Tell her to keep up the good work."

"Will do, thanks."

I smiled at her.

She rolled her eyes and sighed as she pushed me up to critical care.

I thanked her when she took me into Billy's room. It was much darker than mine and he had more machines than me, beeping and booping, and doing their part to keep him alive.

I wheeled over to his bedside and studied him. There were tubes going in and out of various places and the right side of his face was bandaged.

"What did I do to you?" I said feeling tears well up in my eyes.

He stirred and glanced at me. For a long moment, he didn't say or do anything. I was worried he would blame me for everything. Which of course, I was to blame. I never should've hired him for this insane job. I should've retired and moved to that yacht in the middle of the ocean.

He blinked hard and stared at me again. This time he smiled.

"Hey, boss," he said. "How ya doin?"

"I'm doing fine," I said fighting back tears. "How are you?"

"They have me on some stuff that's messing with my head," he said. "I keep seeing things."

"Like what?"

"I don't know, just weird stuff," he said. "People going in and out at all hours of the night."

"Yeah, that's normal," I said. "They have to keep an eye on you."

"Oh, speaking of eyes," he said making me cringe. "You should see my eye."

He pressed a button, so the head of his bed came up a little making it easier for him to talk to me.

"I've got this cool scar that looks like I've been in a fight with Wolverine."

"Who's Wolverine?"

"You're kidding, right? Only the coolest superhero."

"If you say so, kid."

"So, when are we getting back to work?"

My jaw dropped.

"What are you talking about?"

"You know," he said looking around and lowering his voice. "Finding our next cryptid."

"You're in a hospital bed being kept alive by machines," I said. "Your cryptid hunting days are over."

"What? Why?" he said with disappointment glittering in his eye.

"Because I was wrong. I don't need someone helping me do this, I need to retire."

"No way! Just when I get started?"

"And nearly get ended at the same time."

"I mean, yeah, I got a little scratched up, but it's not like I died or anything."

"Actually, you did," came a deep, resonant voice from the doorway.

I turned and in walked a tall man in a lab coat who exuded confidence with every step.

"You were dead for thirty-six seconds while we were working on you," the man said, stopping at the end of the bed, picking up a clipboard, and glancing at it.

"So, Dolores was right," I said to myself more than anyone.

"Who's Dolores?" Billy said.

"That's not important right now," I said. "The doctor's right, you could've died, and you did die."

"But I'm not dead," Billy said. "They brought me back, and I'm ready to go."

Billy tried to sit up straighter but winced in pain and settled back.

"Yeah, I can see how ready you are," I said sarcastically. "You'll be a great help out there in a wheelchair. I can picture it now, you rolling off a cliff or getting tangled in some brambles while... "

I suddenly remembered the outsider in the room.

He stared at me as if waiting for the rest of the sentence, but I clamped my mouth shut.

"I see you've sustained some injuries as well," the doctor said looking at me. "What exactly do the two of you do, 'out there'?"

"Park Ranger," I said at the same time Billy said, "Cryptid hunter."

The doctor's eyes narrowed. He slowly observed Billy, then me.

I laughed.

"What a jokester," I said. "This kid and his imagination. I've told you to quit watching those movies. You get all full of ideas and start seeing things that aren't there."

"Oh, yeah," Billy said, catching me glaring at him while I talked. "I must've gotten confused. I fell asleep watching a werewolf movie and fell off the couch."

"You sustained these injuries falling off a couch?" the doctor said slowly.

"Yep," Billy said, nodding hesitantly as if trying to convince himself.

I chuckled nervously.

"No, of course he didn't," I said. "We were out on a trail when an animal attacked."

"A werewolf?" the doctor said.

"No," I said at the same time Billy said, "Yes."

I shot him another glare.

"I meant it was a *wolf* that attacked, and I wasn't sure *where* it came from," Billy said.

'Nice save,' I thought.

The doctor stared at us one at a time. His eyes seemed to penetrate mine as though he was reading my thoughts.

"At any rate, I recommend that both of you give serious thought to finding new careers," he said. "Or at least taking a long break from… whatever it is you do."

"Sounds like good advice to me," I said.

Billy didn't say anything. He lay in bed and sulked.

"Thank you, doctor… ?" I said, extending my hand.

"Roan," he said, shaking it. "Try to avoid any further contact with werewolves. I hear they can be very anti-social."

"We'll do our best," I said as he left the room.

I sunk into my wheelchair and sighed.

"What the hell is wrong with you?" I said to Billy.

"What did I do now?" he said.

"Cryptid hunter?" I said watching the door to be sure no one else was sneaking in. "Werewolf? Fell off the couch?"

"What? I panicked," he said.

"Really?" I said, sarcastically. "I never would've guessed."

"You know," Billy said straightening with a gleam in his eye. "You're gonna have to make sure I don't run my mouth or say anything stupid around people."

"What are you getting at?" I said narrowing my eyes at him.

"I mean if I were to accidentally go on the news and tell people that we hunt cryptids and how profitable it is, the park would be flooded with cryptid hunters trying to cash in."

"You wouldn't," I said, wincing at the cliché.

"Of course, if I was still employed as your partner, then I would have to keep my mouth shut," he said grinning from ear to ear.

"First off, who ever said you were a partner?" I said. "You're like… "

"Robin?" he said.

"No, you're more like Robin's dog."

His face fell.

"That's not very cool."

"Who said anything about being cool?" I said. "This job is dirty, bloody, and nasty, there's nothing cool about it."

"You don't think that hunting legendary creatures that most people don't even think exist is cool?"

I stared at him. It was the smartest thing I'd heard him say.

"What if I just decide to quit?"

He shrugged.

"Then I'll do it on my own."

I laughed.

"You wouldn't last two minutes against a cryptid."

"I lasted against a werewolf," he said folding his arms across his chest.

"Yeah, because you had help," I said.

He grinned at me.

I hung my head.

"I walked right into that one," I said. "Fine, we'll keep going. But only after we've healed up and gotten some better equipment."

He leaned back and closed his eye.

"Sounds good to me."

Before I knew it, he was snoring. I shook my head and started back down to my own room, stifling a yawn.

A few days later I was strong enough to check myself out of the hospital against medical advice, as usual. I returned home to a construction crew hard at work. I stepped out of the truck and hobbled towards the house with the help of the cane they insisted I take with me.

The inside of the house had made a drastic transformation. The old furniture was gone. In its place was a modern office and a hospital room fully stocked with two beds. On the other side of the hall was an armory, bathroom, and kitchen which had seen surprisingly few renovations.

I hobbled upstairs to find three modern bedrooms, a bathroom, and a communications room. In the basement, the open space had been taken up by two laboratories. The second one contained the secret door to the tunnel leading outside. The triggers were changed slightly and the tunnel had lights installed in the ceiling along the entire length.

I went back upstairs and found the project manager.

I sat in the chair in my new office and let her show me all the enhancements that had been made to the house.

"I've had crews working around the clock just like you stated so that it would be done in under a week. Of course, the extra enhancements have been built with a handful of workers and kept on a need-to-know basis," she said. "I don't think they knew what they were really building."

"Good, I'd like to keep it that way," I said. "So, you're nearly done?"

"Yes, just a little work left to do and then clean up."

"Excellent," I said, pulling a gun out of my pocket and aiming it at her.

She stared at it for a long moment.

"You're the only one who knew what all the secret work was, correct?"

She nodded slowly, her wide eyes still staring at the gun.

"So, if I want to keep my secrets, I need to eliminate you."

She swallowed hard.

"If that's what you feel you have to do, then do it," she said. "But I feel you'd be wasting an opportunity should you ever have a need for such modifications in the future."

"No begging for your life?" I said. "No threats of repercussions or being found out?"

She shook her head slowly.

I smiled and tossed the gun on the desk.

"Well done," I said. "I definitely have a place for you in my organization."

"Excuse me?" she said still staring at the gun.

"You handled yourself professionally under duress and didn't stoop to any threatening or emotional tactics to save yourself."

She narrowed her eyes at me, picked up the gun, and pulled the slide back.

"Empty," she said in a hollow voice.

"I'm not a monster," I said. "I just wanted to see what you're made of."

She tossed the gun back on the desk and stood.

"This is what I'm made of," she said walking out the door.

I struggled to my feet and hobbled after her as quickly as I could.

"Oh, come on," I shouted after her. "You're really gonna let a little thing like being threatened at gunpoint upset you?"

Several of the workers stopped what they were doing and stared at me as I hobbled after her.

She got in her car and started it. I reached the car and stood in front of it, blocking her only exit.

"You don't even want to hear the rest of what I had to say?"

She revved the engine in response.

"You don't want to hear that I was going to give you a hundred-thousand-dollar bonus for your new position?"

She gripped the steering wheel and stared at me but didn't rev the engine. The workers had followed us out of the house and were now standing back at a safe distance, watching the scene unfold.

I stepped around to the driver's side and tapped on her window with my cane.

She kept staring straight ahead but lowered her window a few inches.

"Is that a yes?" I said leaning down.

"One of these days you're going to come across a situation you can't buy your way out of," she said.

"Believe me, I already have," I said.

She sighed heavily, turned off the car, and rolled up her window. She got out, stood toe to toe with me, and slapped me across the face.

I rubbed my stinging cheek.

"Don't you ever point a gun at me again! Loaded or not, are we clear?"

"Crystal."

She walked past me and went back into the house. The workers stared at me for a moment then straggled back into the house as well.

Finally, I hobbled my way back inside. When I made it back to the office, she was at her computer working as though nothing had happened.

"Were the cameras installed as well?" I asked sinking into the chair.

She handed me a spreadsheet of the things I'd asked to be done with the total cost of each item and a checkmark beside it showing that it was completed.

I regarded the list, from the cameras to motion sensors, to all the rest of the measures I'd put in place. There'd be no more surprises... at least not for me.

I pulled out my checkbook, wrote a check to Marie Swanson for one hundred thousand dollars, and handed it to her.

"Here," I said. "After you're done with this job, I want you to take a vacation before coming to work for me."

"Aren't I already working for you?"

"True, but in a part-time status. This is for when you come to work for me full time."

"I'm just not sure what I'd do."

"Manage my finances, along with any other jobs I might need facilitated."

"Sounds rather vague."

I shrugged.

"Nature of the beast," I said. "I'll pay you two hundred thousand a year plus a percentage of any money you make for me."

She narrowed her eyes at me.

"What percentage?"

"How about twenty?"

"How about thirty?"

"How about twenty-five?"

"How about you've got a deal?" she said extending her hand across the desk.

I smiled, reached over, and shook it.

"Now if you don't mind, I've got some work to finish up before I start my vacation."

"You're kicking me out of my own office?" I said.

"I'd just like to finish my work without anyone pulling a gun on me," she said with a sideways look.

I sighed.

"I'm never gonna hear the end of that, am I?"

"Nope."

I got up, left the office, went to my bedroom, and fell into a deep sleep.

***

The next day I drove to the ranger's station. As soon as I walked in the door I was accosted.

"Where the hell have you been?" Ron said.

"In the hospital," I said glancing at my cane. "Why?"

"Dell's gone missing," Sharon said narrowing her eyes at me. "The day after you broke into his office."

'So much for paying her to keep quiet,' I thought.

"Where is he?" Nancy said.

"I have no clue," I said semi-truthfully. I really didn't know where The Man kept his toys once I handed them over.

"We've been combing the park looking for him for the last week," Jeff said. "We thought maybe he fell into a ravine or something."

"When was the last time any of you saw Dell out in the park?" I said. "If he was here, he was always in his office."

"I guess he's right," Ron said, grudgingly. "Dell wasn't much for going into the park. He usually sent one of us."

Then I realized what an opportunity I was missing.

"Tell you what," I said to them. "If it means that much to you, I'll help search the park for him."

They all stared at me and then my cane.

"No offense," Nancy said. "But how much help are you going to be limping around on a cane?"

"I can drive around and search," I said. "I can also hire a search and rescue team."

"At your own expense?" Sharon said.

"It doesn't look like the state cares very much," I said. "Have they sent anyone?"

"They did send this guy," Jeff said. "They said he was an expert tracker. But he's really creepy and hasn't checked in for days. In fact, he could be missing as well."

"Ok," I said. "I'll hire a team and have them start looking tomorrow. In the meantime, who's been in charge?"

They all shot glances at one another.

"Well, who is it?" I said.

"Actually, you," Ron said. "Once Dell was reported missing, they sent orders that you were to take over. Jeff's been doing it since you were out on leave."

Jeff stepped up and handed me a set of keys.

"I guess you're the boss now," he said.

I focused on the keys, then their expectant eyes.

"I actually came here to turn in my resignation," I said.

Jeff's eyes lit up immediately.

"But I think I'll stick around to make sure this search is done right," I said, watching Jeff's face fall.

"What do you mean?" Sharon said.

"I mean you have a man who's been missing for days yet here you all stand in the office doing nothing," I said. "Get out there and find him!"

They stared at me in shock, then filed out one by one.

I went to Dell's office, unlocked the door this time, went in, sat in the chair, then put my feet up on his former desk. I smiled broadly thinking about sending those idiots out on a wild Dell hunt.

I was busy being pleased with myself when the front door opened and closed. For a long moment, nothing happened. I thought maybe one of my idiots had forgotten something, but I didn't hear them come the rest of the way into the station. It seemed like they were just standing in the doorway. It was around the corner so I couldn't see, but swear I heard sniffing.

I was about to get up and see what was happening when a face appeared in my door.

I jumped causing my leg to flop down on the floor painfully.

The man standing there stared at me, then slowly lifted his hand and knocked on the glass. He seemed weathered as if he'd been left out in the elements too long.

I motioned him inside.

"Who are you?" I said.

"I might ask you the same question," he said slowly with a voice that sounded like gravel.

"You might, but I asked first, so I won't answer until you do."

He took a step towards the desk, and I found my hand involuntarily drifting toward my gun.

"Mind if I sit?" he said.

I gestured toward the chair, and he glided into it slowly like releasing a hydraulic lift.

"I take it you're the new boss," he said.

"It would appear so," I said, feeling the hair on the back of my neck stand on end.

He chuckled.

"You seem to be a step up from the rest of those bootlickers."

"I still haven't heard who you are or what you're doing here."

"Yes, you have," he said, leering at me. "You just haven't heard it from me."

"Ok then, let's hear it from you," I said, resting my hand on my pistol.

"The state sent me to search for your boss."

"Well then, you better get searching."

"I have," he said. "He's not here."

"Then where is he?"

He leaned forward just a bit.

"You know," he said.

Beads of sweat started forming on my forehead.

"I have no idea," I lied. "I've been on leave in the hospital."

"About that," he said. "You seem to be quite accident-prone lately."

"What do you mean?"

"You've been in the hospital four times in the last few months. Having some health issues?"

"As a matter of fact, yes. Not that it's any of your business."

He smiled.

"Hunting cryptids will do that."

I glared at him and tightened the grip on my gun.

Without warning, he rose smoothly out of the chair and left.

I turned and stared out the window to see which vehicle he got into, but he was gone.

I released my white knuckles from the gun, then pulled out a handkerchief and wiped my forehead.

'Did that really happen?' I thought.

Chapter 8

I slammed on the brakes and the dust cloud that had been following my truck continued on in front of it as I got out, hobbled to the small stone house and knocked on the door.

It opened and I proceeded inside, knowing I wouldn't find my host behind the door.

"Dolores!" I called.

"What's wrong," she said from behind me, causing me to do a painful little dance of fright.

"Well, that was unnecessary," I said grasping my leg and limping over to the comfy chair.

"Sorry, I thought I'd give you a bit of a jump start," she said smiling. "How have you been?"

"Super," I said sarcastically. "I just won the gold in the thousand-meter sprint."

"Wow, you are feeling nasty today."

"I just had an encounter in the park ranger station."

"What do you mean, an encounter?"

"With a cryptid."

She sat on her couch, her face suddenly serious.

"Tell me everything," she said.

I told her what had happened with the rangers and the so-called tracker.

"Describe him," she said closing her eyes.

"He was a little taller than me, he was lean, weathered, and walked with a slow, no not slow, it was a deliberate walk like he was stalking me as prey."

"What color was his skin?" she said.

"That's a little racist, don't you think?"

"Just answer the question."

"It seemed a little on the reddish side," I said. "I just took it for a sunburn."

She sighed and opened her eyes.

"Well, my friend, it looks like you may have been visited by a skinwalker."

"One of those that can change form?"

She nodded.

"Then why didn't he attack while we were alone?" I said. "He knew who I was. He even called me a cryptid hunter."

"Isn't it obvious?" she said. "He's toying with you. He wants you to know he can get to you anytime he wants."

"But why?" I said. "What did I do to him?"

She shrugged.

"Who knows with skinwalkers? They're an unpredictable bunch. Maybe he sees a worthy adversary."

"Fine then," I said. "Bring it on. I've taken down bigger prey."

"You don't understand," she said. "It's not like those others you stumbled across. This creature is hunting you. He's on high alert, probably watching your every move. There's literally no place you can go that he won't find you. He probably knows you're here right now."

The panicked look in my eye lasted for a second before morphing into determination.

"Fine, I'll go hole up and wait for him to come to me."

She shook her head.

"You're not dealing with some dumb animal that will blunder into one of your traps. This is an alpha predator. The fact that he's still alive shows he has skill at concealing himself."

I leaned back in my seat; unaware I'd been sitting on the edge.

"So, what do I do?" I said.

"I don't know."

We sat there in silence for a handful of moments before I painfully rose out of the chair and started for the door.

"What are you going to do?" she said.

"I don't know," I said. "I'll figure something out. I always do."

I shot her a smile that was meant to be cute and disarming, but I knew it didn't reach my eyes.

She smiled back, but it was full of worry.

I stepped out of the house, and something felt wrong. It was in the air. There was no sound, no wind, nothing. It felt like nature was holding its breath waiting to see what was about to happen.

I stepped toward the truck, hand on my pistol, looking all around for whatever unnatural thing was lurking about.

I saw the most disturbing thing I could see…

Nothing.

I stepped over to my truck, checking around the side before approaching the door. It was covered in dirt from the drive here. When I reached for the latch, I saw it.

Right in the middle of the door was a large pawprint.

I whipped around, gun in hand, knowing with every ounce of instinct in me that he was standing behind me, waiting to strike.

Nothing was there.

I aimed the gun around, breathing hard, but there was nothing.

I slowly backed into the truck, closed and locked the door, then drove home like a bat out of hell.

I pulled in and slid to a stop right in front of my project manager.

"What the hell?" she said dusting herself off.

I jumped out of the truck and nearly fell, then turned back and grabbed my cane.

"Are all the security measures up and working?" I said limping into the house as fast as I could.

"Yes, they can be enabled whenever you want to test them," she said trying to keep up with me.

"Turn them on, all of them, right now," I said.

"There are still workers in a couple of areas cleaning up," she said. "They could get caught in the traps."

"Then get them out and turn on my security," I snapped.

She grabbed my arm and turned me around to face her, almost making me fall.

"What's going on?" she said looking deeply into my eyes.

"You don't want to know," I said heading for the basement.

I went into the second lab and triggered the secret door. I hobbled at a blistering pace to the end of the tunnel. When I got there, I made sure the lock was secure, then breathed a sigh of relief as I made my way back to the lab a little slower than I had come.

When I closed the secret entrance and came out of the lab, she was there waiting for me, arms folded across her chest.

"Everyone's out, everything's turned on," she said. "Now tell me what's happening."

"Listen, Marie, may I call you Marie?" I said.

"Ms. Swanson will do," she said coldly.

"Right, Ms. Swanson, I can't tell you what's going on, but I can tell you I'm in a considerable amount of danger. And if you don't leave immediately, you'll be in danger as well."

She shot me a skeptical look.

"Is this another test?" she said.

"I promise you on all that's holy, it's not," I said, holding up my right hand. "You need to leave, right now."

She stood still as a statue.

"Ok, if I wasn't nursing a gimp leg, I would pick you up and carry you to your car," I said. "You're not understanding how serious the situation is."

"So, tell me."

I sighed.

"Fine, there's an alpha predator on his way here, he may even be here already, and I don't know what he's going to do."

"An alpha predator?"

"Fine, a skinwalker," I said. "Do you know what a skinwalker is?"

"Yes," she said with a far-off look.

"So, you know how dangerous it is, and you need to leave."

She turned without a word and disappeared up the stairs. I followed and watched as she bolted out the door into her car and left a trail of dust on the way down the long driveway.

I breathed a sigh of relief as I closed and locked the door. Then went to my office and double-checked that all the security measures were armed.

I had barely sat in my chair until an alarm sounded on my computer. I switched to the camera for that area and there he was, walking just as calmly as you please. He was near the tree that served as the hidden entrance. He stood beside it, sniffed it, then examined it paying close attention to the trunk.

After a minute or so he ceased his investigation, stared straight into the camera, smiled, then walked away.

I tried to switch cameras and see which direction he went, but he had disappeared.

I went to the armory and grabbed my pistol, then called Dolores.

"He's baiting you," she said. "He wants to rattle you, so you'll be on edge."

"It's working," I said.

"You can't let it. If he gets under your skin, you could panic and then he has you."

"Well thank you Ms. Sunshine for that cheery thought."

"I know you're trying to keep things light, but I'm telling you, this might be the one time you have to go lethal. Thomas might not be able to save you if you panic."

"What do I do then?"

"Use your money," she said. "You like to do that. Look up weapons to use against Skinwalkers then have some sent to your house."

"Don't you know what they are?"

"I've heard rumors, but you should get some scientific fact."

"About skinwalkers?" I said. "I'll get laughed off the internet if I try to buy skinwalker weapons."

"You might be surprised what you'll find."

"Alright," I said. "You be safe too. When I left your place I had the strange feeling I was being watched."

"I'll make sure to lock the door," she said.

"You might want to do more than that."

"Believe me," she said in a lower voice. "No one gets into this house without my permission."

I fought off the chills that ran down my spine.

"Ok, well I'm off to batten down the hatches."

"Good luck," she said.

"I always have good luck," I said.

"Here's hoping it doesn't run out."

She hung up leaving me staring at the phone and wondering when the day would come that I did run out of luck. I thought it had been when Dell attacked, but I somehow managed to survive that one too.

Was my life really a ticking time bomb? Did it really matter if I tried to retire or not? Or would I end up like John Wick, constantly being dragged back in?

I made sure the security measures were all armed, then sat back and tried to think of some way to relax.

"I'm gonna go eat some pop-tarts," I said to myself, very aware of how empty the house was.

I checked my cell phone to make sure it was fully charged and the security app was set to notifications so I would get an alert if any alarms sounded.

I had two packs of blueberry pop-tarts and a glass of milk, then went to bed and fell asleep watching episodes of Red vs. Blue on Youtube.

***

I woke and scanned around the dark room. Panic gripped me until I remembered where I was. There was a noise that I couldn't seem to locate. I glanced around and saw something blurry light-up red. I rubbed my eyes and looked again. It was my phone.

There was an alert. Someone was setting off my motion sensors.

I sat bolt upright sending pain shooting down my injured leg.

"Son of a… " I said as another alarm went off, then another.

I stared at the phone and the three alarms were going off in completely different locations. The first was at the far end of the driveway, the second was near the tunnel entrance, and the third was at the front door.

I got up, threw on a robe, grabbed my pistol out of the nightstand, and went out to see what was happening.

I struggled down the steps, regretting that I had left my cane beside the bed. Until I made it to the bottom, I was breathing hard. Holding my gun in my off-hand so I could use the railing for support, I reached the bottom and stared at the front door.

Looking at the phone, there was still an intruder alert sounding for it. I switched to the camera and saw nothing. Switching to the other two cameras showed nothing as well.

'I guess I need to reset the sensitivity,' I thought seeing that the wind was blowing leaves around. I chuckled and turned toward the kitchen when I heard it and froze.

There was a soft scratching sound coming from the front door. I turned, half expecting it to crash in and my attacker come rushing up on me. But it didn't. I looked at the camera again and this time I saw a dark form.

It was large and hairy, like a wolf, only bigger. It was scratching near the doorknob as though it would tear through the wood and release the latch.

I aimed the gun at the door and flicked the safety off. Then I had another thought. 'Why not use all this technology I've paid for?'

I tapped the screen on the phone and enlarged the front door. With a tap on an icon, a solid steel door slid down and landed with a thud. It covered the entire entrance in a barrier it would take a tank to get through.

I scrutinized the camera and saw the wolf look up at it.

I gave the phone the finger, knowing there was no way the creature would see it, but it made me feel better.

The wolf stalked around to the side of the house. I followed him with the cameras as he searched for weaknesses.

I grinned as a thought occurred to me.

I dialed The Man and only had to wait a few seconds until he answered.

"Yes?" he said.

"Are you interested in a skinwalker?"

"Of course," he said. "Are you in immediate danger?"

"No, I'm inside the house and he's outside."

"We're on our way," he said.

Eight minutes later I heard helicopters land in the front yard.

I opened the front door to The Man standing there waiting.

"Well?" he said.

I glanced at my phone.

"The last I saw him, he was near the rear corner of the house," I said pointing in the direction of the camera.

The Man flicked his fingers and four soldiers disappeared around either side of the house, moving silently.

"So does this mean we're on speaking terms again?" The Man said.

"Don't get too cocky," I said with a grin. "Let's see how this goes."

I could see the edge of his mouth starting to rise into a grin when the soldiers returned.

"No sign, sir," the lead soldier said.

His mouth curved downward.

"Did you check the field?"

"Yes, sir, no sign."

He turned toward me, and all traces of humor or lightheartedness were gone.

"So, this was a prank?" he said. "A little payback for being late?"

"No, I swear, it was there," I said involuntarily taking a step back at the ferocity of his emotional change.

I scrolled through the cameras until I reached the front door then rewound the video.

"See, here it is," I said showing the video of the wolf at the door.

He observed the video then glared at me.

"Next time you call," he said. "It better not be because a stray dog woke you from your beauty sleep."

He turned and stormed out the front door, followed closely by the soldiers. Within a minute they were gone. The only thing left was the wind current from their chopper blades.

"Well, crap," I said as I stood there on the front porch watching them go and wondering to myself if I had really seen it when something in the tree line moved.

It was big, black, and coming at me fast.

I dove inside, slammed the door, and tried to lock it, but the wolf was already there pushing against me with inhuman strength. It knocked me down, but I planted both my feet against the door and pushed with everything I had. My injured leg was screaming for me to stop, but I knew that would be catastrophic.

I floundered, not knowing what to do, losing ground by the second, when I saw the phone lying on the floor. I reached for it, but it was just out of reach. I scooted toward it, knowing I would lose ground and the door would be that much closer to opening.

The screen was still up for the front door defenses. I held my breath for a moment, closed my eyes, and concentrated.

I rolled away from the door at the same time I pressed the button.

The wolf used his strength to lunge inside at the same time the steel door came slamming down. It destroyed the wooden front door, just missing my injured leg and slamming into the wolf's back, pinning him to the floor.

I sat up and spotted the now trapped wolf still snarling and tearing at the floor trying to get inside.

I painfully rose and pulled out my gun.

"Oh well," I said, aiming at the wolf's head. "I won't get paid, but I won't have to worry about you either."

I pulled the trigger.

The wolf howled in pain but kept coming.

I stared at the gun as if it was the problem.

"If at first you don't succeed," I said. "Try, try again."

I pulled the trigger every time I said try, but he was still coming. I went for broke and unloaded the clip into him, but it only seemed to make him madder. In fact, he was inching his way inside.

"Time to go," I said, hobbling toward the basement door.

I had just made it to the bottom of the steps when I heard the steel door thump against the floor.

"Gotta move, gotta move," I told myself pushing my injured leg to its limit as I ran to the second lab.

The basement door exploded as I opened the secret entrance. I just got a glimpse of the wolf as the door began to shut.

"Come on, come on!" I yelled, willing the door to shut faster.

It closed as I heard a thump against it that shook the wall. I pressed a button on the phone that closed the lab door and locked it. Then I started walking down the long tunnel and back to the house. I was greeted by the metal security door. I tapped an icon and the door slid back up into the wall. There was no front door left, only splinters.

I stepped down the basement stairs and came to the second lab. The walls had been ripped to shreds in places near the doors, but the reinforced steel bars that were hidden behind the drywall did their job of keeping him inside.

I peeked in through one of the holes and the wolf snarled at me, clawing out through the exposed drywall toward me. But I was back far enough to be out of reach.

I stood there watching him.

After a while, he settled down and realized he couldn't get to me. He laid down and transformed back into his human form.

"Where am I?" he said looking around the room.

"You're in my basement," I said.

"What have you done to me?" he said.

"I've captured you."

"What will you do now?"

"Well, I haven't had a barbeque for a while," I said. "I wonder how tough wolf meat is."

"What?" he said. "You wouldn't."

"You terrorized me, destroyed my house, tried to kill me, who knows how many other people you've done the same or worse to, all in the name of tracking people and helping them," I said. "Tell me again what I wouldn't do."

He stepped away from the bars and snarled at me, then said some word in a language I didn't understand. I assumed it was a curse.

"Gesundheit," I said to the wolf as I dialed The Man.

"What?" he said.

"I have a pickup for you."

Silence.

"Don't waste my time."

"I'm not, I really have a pickup for you."

"I'm not coming back there tonight."

"I'll tell you what," I said. "I'll bet you my fee. If you come back and there's not a cryptid here, I'll pay you my normal fee out of my own account."

Silence.

"You better not be playing a game or you'll lose more than money."

"I swear I have a cryptid."

He sighed.

"We'll be there soon."

Twenty minutes later The Man and his soldiers met me at the door.

"This way, gentlemen," I said, leading them down into the basement as we made our way past the remnants of the door.

We approached the second lab and I didn't see anyone there.

The Man glared at me.

"He's in there," I said, as one of the soldiers went around the side.

"Sir," he said.

The Man stepped around to the side and saw a naked man curled up in the fetal position, shivering.

"Please don't hurt me anymore!" he screamed when he saw me.

I laughed, but The Man didn't.

"Come on," I said. "It's obviously a ploy."

"Help me," he said. "This guy picked me up on the street, then tied me up and brought me here. He said he had to have something to deliver tonight."

"This is the wolf I showed you on the camera," I said.

"I apologize, sir," The Man said to him. "We'll get you out of there."

"No, you can't," I said. "He's dangerous."

"Open it," The Man ordered.

"No."

"Open it!"

"You don't know what you're doing."

He grabbed the phone from me and tapped an icon that opened the door.

He tossed me back my phone and covered the man with his coat. The soldiers escorted him out. He shook and whimpered when they took him past me. Then he turned toward me and smiled.

"Oh shit," I said, ducking back into the ruined lab and slamming the door closed.

I watched in horror as he transformed back into the wolf and slashed at the soldier helping him.

The room exploded into bedlam as soldiers were caught in their own line of sight. They couldn't fire at him for fear of hitting their own men. In the meantime, the wolf already had two soldiers down and was holding The Man by his throat.

The soldiers outflanked him and fired into his side, but it was no good. He roared in pain but didn't go down. They fired tranquilizer darts into him, but they were ineffective to his wolf form.

The Man struggled against him, punching and kicking like a man possessed. He managed to break free but received a vicious slash across the throat as payment. He went down hard. I saw him holding his throat as he lay on the floor with a puddle of blood rapidly expanding under him.

I had to do something. I scrolled through my phone and searched the park ranger's database. After what seemed like forever, but was probably only a few seconds, I found the information I needed.

"Tokala Lapahie!" I screamed at the top of my lungs.

The wolf froze. As if in slow motion, he toppled over and lay still.

I opened the door and hobbled over to The Man. He was conscious but unable to speak.

"You two," I said pointing at two relatively uninjured soldiers. "Get him back in the lab."

I pointed at the wolf that was barely breathing. They dragged him back inside and dropped him none too gently, then came out and locked the door.

"We need to get him to a hospital," one of the soldiers said hovering over The Man.

"No time," I said. "Follow me."

They picked him up and followed along as we went upstairs and to the end of the hall where the room was set up like a hospital room.

The medic who had followed along with us took over.

"Do you have any plasma," she said, trying to patch the wound that was still spouting blood.

"Over here," I showed her.

She worked like a woman possessed, ordering soldiers to perform certain tasks to assist her. I stayed in the background out of the way but accessible if they needed to know where anything was.

In the meantime, two of the other injured soldiers were brought up and tended to.

I sat in a chair, not realizing just how tired I was, and fell asleep.

Sometime later, I was awakened by a gentle nudge. I looked up into the tired eyes of the medic.

"How is he?" I said.

"He's resting," she said. "He'll make it, thanks to you."

"You're the one who deserves the credit," I said.

"No, he never would've made it to a hospital. If you hadn't had these supplies here… Anyway, the guys and I are kinda hungry, do you mind if we raid your fridge?"

"Not at all," I said. "In fact, I think I'll join you."

She helped me up out of the chair then I offered my arm. She hooked hers through mine and escorted me to the kitchen.

We all sat there around the kitchen table, exhausted, eating Cheetos and drinking soda like we were taking a break from a movie marathon. I rose and told them they were welcome to anything in the house, including the bedrooms if they needed a nap.

I recommended feeding the downstairs guest, but the consensus was that he could starve and burn in hell.

***

I got up a few hours later, feeling refreshed as I watched the sunrise. I went down to the medical wing and found The Man awake and alert.

"Have you been enjoying your stay here at Che' ranger?" I said in a fake French voice.

He chuckled.

"The accommodations are adequate," he said in a voice just above a whisper.

"You insult me, misère," I said. "I shall have you removed from my presence at once."

"I think I'm being removed soon anyway," he said. "This was a great idea, to dedicate a room to urgent care."

I shrugged.

"Just sick of doctors telling me what to do," I said. "If they work for me, I get to tell them what to do."

"Except me," the medic said walking into the room with a tray of donuts.

She sat the tray on the table and then offered one to The Man and me.

I held up my donut.

"A toast," I said. "To misunderstandings."

"And apologies," The Man said holding up his donut, looking at me.

"And to living long enough to see them through," the medic added as we touched our donuts together.

We all bit into our treats and enjoyed a moment of peace.

"I think we should all go on vacation together," I said. "I know this great place on the Mediterranean."

"As tempting as that is," The Man said. "You know you're not my only hunter. I have to be on call 24/7 for when they need me."

"God only knows what would happen if you didn't show up when one called," I said.

"God only knows," he agreed.

"Just to be sure, we are good aren't we?" I said.

He held up his hand and I shook it.

"We're better than good," he said. "I owe you my life."

I smiled.

"Damn straight."

We all chuckled.

"Just out of curiosity," he said. "How did you stop him?"

"I said his name," I said. "It's a skinwalker thing. If you say their name, it hurts them or they lose power or something like that."

"But, how did you know his name?" the medic asked.

"I searched it on my phone," I said. "He was sent by the park ranger service, so all I had to do was see who was on assignment at our station."

"And his name was listed in the records," The Man said. "Ingenious."

"Well, I can't take all the credit," I said. "Someone else identified him as a skinwalker for me."

"Dolores," he said with a far-off look.

"That's right," I said. "What's the deal with you two anyway?"

"We have… a history," he said.

"And that history is… ?"

"Can you keep a secret," he said leaning slightly closer.

"Yeah," I whispered.

"So can I," he said, then sat back up and grinned at me.

"Ok, smartass," I said. "I guess I'll have to wait until one of you is ready to fess up."

"Well, then you're in for a long wait," he said.

***

The next day we all marched down to the basement. The Man carried a tranq gun and the soldiers had stun nets.

Tokala was in human form and was looking a little worse for wear.

"Please you have to help me," he said to The Man. "I've been left down here to starve."

He took a step closer to the bars.

"You think I give a damn about whether they gave you a sandwich when you nearly ripped my throat out?"

"But this is cruelty, this is mistreatment, you can't get away with this."

"I can get away with whatever I want," The Man said. "And guess what, you're going to be a guest at my facility from now on."

Tokala cringed as he stared at the gun.

The Man glanced from him to me.

"Would you like to do the honors?" he said offering me the gun.

"Absolutely," I said taking it from him. "Any last words?"

"What? What's in that gun? You can't just kill me in captivity. I'll notify the humane society… "

I aimed and shot him in the crotch.

He doubled over, squealing in pain for a long moment, then fell silent.

"Whoops," I said. "Did I do that?"

Fifteen minutes later I watched as the two helicopters flew away.

I dialed my travel agent and booked the first flight to Venice.

Chapter 9

They say time heals all wounds. I truly believe that. Of course, lounging on the deck of a yacht with my two favorite lovely ladies on either side of me, looking out over the crystal-clear Mediterranean doesn't hurt either.

I sighed a deep sigh of contentment.

Why in the world would I ever want to go back?

I thought of the times I'd been injured, the times that a mere fraction of an inch could've ended my life. I thought of the idiots I pretended to work with and my psychotic boss who had suddenly turned into a werewolf.

Didn't see that one coming.

I thought of Dolores and Billy, of how much I enjoyed being out in the woods with no one to tell me what to do.

And then it hit me. The answer I'd been looking for all this time.

I enjoyed risking my life.

Just like a skydiver, a race car driver, or those kids I've seen recording themselves walking on top of skyscrapers. I liked being chased. For me there's no more pure adrenaline rush than being scared out of my wits, knowing that there's a creature stalking me that could shred me into tiny little pieces in the most horrific way.

My mind settled in and accepted the thought. The more it sank in, the more sense it made.

I leaned back in contentment, having one of the great questions answered made me feel even more at ease. I could've melted right through the mesh in the chair.

So, this is what inner peace felt like. I'd heard people blather on about it. Most times I just ignored them and went on with my miserable life. Maybe this was what Dolores was talking about with being who you were meant to be.

One of the ladies beside me stirred from her nap. She eyed me and smiled, then started rubbing my bare chest. After a minute she got up, reached her hand down and helped me up, then guided me inside. I watched the bikini bottom, which barely kept her butt covered, wiggle back and forth with each step she took.

She slid the door open, stepped inside, and threw herself on the couch.

I slid the door shut and joined her.

Yeah, there were some other aspects of inner peace that I rather enjoyed.

***

On my flight home, I stared out over the ocean and realized for the first time I was looking forward to going back to work. The thought startled and amused me at the same time.

'I guess there's no turning back now,' I thought. 'I'm a cryptid hunter, for better or worse.'

Worse made me think of all the times I'd been injured, which in turn made me think of Billy.

'I wonder how he's doing. Maybe I should've checked on him during my recuperation.'

I remembered I needed to find a doctor to hire on an on-call status. The only reason The Man was alive was because his medic had been there. I needed someone I could call on a moment's notice.

That doctor who questioned Billy and me in his room sprang to mind. But I wasn't sure how to track him down, or more importantly, if he could be trusted.

I would have to look into that.

I pulled up a note app on my phone and typed in 'To do list'. The first entry was, 'find doctor', followed by, 'check on Billy' and, 'find next cryptid'. After a moment's thought, I added, 'Check on idiot park rangers.'

With Dell gone, I guess I really was responsible for them. It would be easy to just quit and tell the park service to send someone else to keep these buffoons in line. But some part of me really wanted to keep tormenting them… I mean, keep an eye on them to make sure they were safe, yeah, that's it.

When I landed, I hopped in my truck and drove over to the hospital. I approached the front desk and asked for Billy.

"What's Billy's last name?" the receptionist said.

I opened my mouth and then realized.

"I don't know."

She raised an eyebrow.

"You don't know the last name of the person you want to check on?"

"It never came up."

"I'm sorry, I can only give out information to family members."

"Ok," I said, pulling out my cell phone and dialing the administrator.

Before it had rung once, I spotted the doctor and headed toward him.

"What's up, doc?" I said.

He stared at me in confusion.

"I'm sorry, do I know you?"

"You should, you treated me."

"I treat a lot of people."

"Ones who had been attacked by a werewolf," I said, leaning forward and lowering my voice.

"Ah yes," he said, his eyes lighting up with recognition. "You and that young man who couldn't seem to get your stories straight."

I glanced around to see if anyone else was listening.

"Yeah, how is he?"

"How is who?"

"My friend, Billy."

"Oh, I believe he's gone."

"He's dead?"

"No, he was released."

"Oh, thank God. I thought… "

"No, he's fine. He should be fully recovered by now and ready to… do whatever it is you really do."

"Speaking of that, do you have some time this afternoon?"

"Why?"

"I wanted to offer you a job."

"I have a job, thanks."

"Not like this."

"Not interested."

"How about if I pay you for your time, just to listen?"

"I don't think so."

I reached into my wallet and pulled out ten one thousand dollar bills.

I handed them to him.

"Just listen to what I have to say, please."

He gazed at the cash, then at me.

"Who are you, really?" he said.

I pulled out a business card that had only numbers on it and held it with the money.

"Come over this afternoon and find out."

He slowly took the money and the card.

I nodded and walked away.

I drove home and was surprised to find a truck in my driveway. I reached into the glove box and pulled out a pistol. I slowly entered the house, checking for the intruder. I would have to upgrade my security if random strangers were making themselves at home.

I continued down the hallway, checking rooms, when I noticed the smell. Someone was cooking.

'That takes a lot of nerve,' I thought heading for the kitchen, madder than I'd been in a while.

I burst in through the door and spotted someone standing by the stove with their back to me.

"Freeze, scumbag!" I said, pointing my gun at him.

He slowly raised his hands and dropped the spatula that was in his hands.

"Good, now turn around, slowly."

He turned around to face me.

"Hiya, boss," Billy said.

"Geez, Billy, scare the hell out of me," I said, sticking the pistol in my waistband. "What're you doing here?"

"You let me pick a room, I assumed I could live here now since it would be easier when we go hunting."

I observed the scars on his face from the last time we went hunting together.

"Ok, kid, whatcha cookin'?" I said.

"Scrambled eggs, you want some?"

"Nah, I'll pass, thanks. I'm gonna go change. I have company coming later."

"More?"

"What do you mean, more?"

"There's been people coming and going through here constantly since I got here."

I panicked for a moment, then the thought hit me.

"Must be the construction crew finishing up some repairs."

"Yeah, I noticed you've made a lot of changes to the place," he said. "Is there anything I should know about?"

"I'll show you the secret passageways later. Right now, I'm gonna go change then head to my office. Enjoy your breakfast."

"Sure thing, boss," he said, grabbing the spatula off the floor and turning back to his eggs.

I walked out of the kitchen and paused.

Should I have told him it was good to see him fully recovered? But he wasn't. He had scars on his face and who knew where else? Was he fully recovered? Could I depend on him when things got dicey?

I shook away those thoughts. Hopefully, we won't have to find out for a while.

I went to my room, changed, and went back down to my office. I opened my computer and checked the balance of my dummy corporation. The amount was a little more than I expected. There were emails from Marie, about the investments she had made and how much money each one was making.

I was happy to see she had taken the challenge seriously.

And speaking of seriously, I swiveled my chair around and unlocked the file cabinet. I pulled out the thick file that I got from Dell, laid it on the desk, and started leafing through it.

With each page, my eyes grew wider. When I was done, I closed the file and sat back. My worldview had been forever changed.

"It can't be real," I said softly, even though I already knew it was. I had personally encountered just a fraction of what was in the file. But my experiences didn't even scratch the surface.

"What can't be real?" Billy said from the doorway.

I jumped in my chair.

"Geez, kid, didn't anyone ever teach you to knock?"

He knocked on the inside of the doorframe.

I narrowed my eyes at him.

"This here town ain't big enough for two smartasses," I said with a half grin. "We're gonna have to do something about that."

He hung his head.

"Am I about to lose some more salary?"

I fought to keep my face straight.

"I'll let you off with a warning this time."

He brightened.

"Cool. So what can't be real?"

"Don't worry about it," I said. "Just more cryptid stuff."

"Shouldn't that worry me? I mean I am your assistant."

"Sidekick."

"I prefer assistant," he said. "It sounds more official. Besides, I'd look horrible in tights."

I chuckled in spite of myself.

"So what's the next mission?" he said.

"Slow down there, I just got back from vacation, you just got out of the hospital. Maybe we could let the supernatural critters infesting this park have a day or two head start before we go on our next hunt."

He gazed at me with a frowny face.

"Don't look at me like that," I said, fighting back a smile. "The answer is no."

"Ok, then how about the tour?"

I reached into the desk drawer and pulled out two plastic cards that looked like credit cards. I handed one to Billy.

"Keep it with you whenever you're in the house."

"Ok," he said looking at it dubiously.

"Follow me," I said getting up and walking toward a very plain-looking corner.

"You see the knot in the wood here on the wall?"

"Yes."

"Anytime you see a knot in the wood, there's a secret entrance nearby."

I tapped my card against the knot and a door slid silently to the side.

"Cool!" Billy said.

"Once opened, you have ten seconds to get inside."

I jumped through the door as it slid shut.

I waited patiently for a few seconds until the door slid open again.

"So you were just going to leave me there?" he said.

"I wanted you to try it on your own."

I turned and started down the hallway that had lights built into the ceiling. They were bright enough to see, but not like broad daylight. We reached a spot where a spiral staircase stood off to the side of the hallway.

"Look here," I said, pointing at a lit plaque mounted on the wall. "It shows you what's in each direction of the hallway and what's up the stairs."

The arrow to the right said, 'Office'. The left arrow said, 'Main entrance', and the one pointing up said, 'Master bedroom.'

My watch beeped. I tapped it and the display showed a car pulling into the driveway.

"We better go this way," I said, pointing left. "We're about to have a guest."

"Were you expecting someone?"

"The doctor from the hospital," I said walking toward the main entrance.

"Which one?"

"The one you almost told about our cryptid hunting."

"Oh," he said.

We reached the end of the hallway, and I tapped the card against the knot on the wall. The door slid open, and we stepped out next to the grandfather clock, just a few feet away from the front door.

"That was cool," Billy said watching as the door slid closed. "Are there any more passageways?"

"Yes, but they'll have to wait for another time."

I opened the door as the doctor was reaching for the doorbell.

He seemed mildly surprised but recovered quickly.

"Good afternoon," he said.

"Good afternoon," I returned. "I'm glad you decided to come."

I stepped aside and ushered him into the main hall.

"Billy," he said with a nod. "Good to see you up and about."

"You too," Billy said, instantly chiding himself for his awkward answer.

The doctor smiled.

I shook my head.

"Would you like to go talk in my office?" I said.

"Of course."

I started toward the office, with the doctor in tow and Billy bringing up the rear.

"This is a nice place you have here," the doctor said.

"Thanks," Billy and I both said at the same time.

I glared at him and he slid over behind the doctor to avoid my eyes.

The doctor grinned as we continued toward the office. When we stepped into the room, I stopped Billy.

"Why don't you go get us some coffee?" I said, then shut the door.

I offered the doctor a seat then went around to the other side of my desk and sat in my chair.

"So, what's this job you'd like to offer me?" he said.

"Straight to the point, I like that," I said. "I need a doctor to be on call 24/7 for emergencies."

"Pass," he said rising out of his seat.

"You don't even want to hear me out?"

"I work full-time at a hospital. I'm on call quite often. I have no desire to be at someone else's beck and call."

"I can pay you more than the hospital."

"I seriously doubt that."

I opened my checkbook and wrote a check for one million dollars.

I sat it on the desk in front of him.

"I'd pay you this much a year just to be on call and be able to be here at a moment's notice."

He gazed at the check.

"How can you afford to pay this just to have someone on call?"

"Don't worry about that."

"No, if I were to work for you, I would want to know exactly what I'm getting into."

I leaned back in my seat and sighed. Just then, Billy came in with the coffee.

"Thank you, Billy," the doctor said, sitting back down.

Billy found a chair by the wall and sat down to listen. I sipped the coffee and then sat it down.

"What do you think we do?" I said, gesturing to Billy while holding the doctor's eyes.

"I really don't know," he said rubbing his chin. "Definitely something dangerous seeing the wounds you both received."

"What kind of danger, in your opinion?" I said, seeing Billy on the edge of his seat like he was bursting to tell the doctor.

"I don't really know," he said. "I can't quite believe the nonsense you two were talking about in the hospital."

Billy's knees were jumping with excitement.

I rolled my eyes.

"Ok, Billy, you can tell him before you pee on the carpet."

I had no sooner finished speaking until he blurted out, "We're cryptid hunters!"

The doctor gaped at him, then at me. He seemed to be judging our expressions to tell if we were serious or not.

"Ok," he said. "You've had your laugh, now how about the truth?"

"It is the truth," I said, pulling out my phone and scrolling through my pictures until I came to the bigfoot I'd captured, lying unconscious on the ground.

I handed him the phone.

"Scroll through as many as you'd like," I said. "That'll show you it's not fake."

He scrolled through picture after picture. His face remained impassive, hiding whatever thoughts he was having. Billy, on the other hand, was still barely holding himself in his chair. Just waiting for the moment to tell the doctor all about our adventures.

The doctor finished scrolling and handed me back the phone.

"This is real?"

"Absolutely!" Billy said. "I was attacked by an honest-to-God werewolf. He nearly killed me."

"I've never seen someone so excited by that prospect," the doctor said.

"That's why we need someone to be here at a moment's notice," I said. "After that attack, when Billy was in the hospital, there was another attack that nearly cost a man his life. If the infirmary hadn't been here along with his medic, he wouldn't be here."

"You went after a cryptid without me?" Billy said.

"I didn't actually go after him," I said rolling my eyes. "He came after me."

Billy's hang-dog expression didn't go away.

"Did you want me to drag you out of your hospital bed and let that thing snack on you?"

"I guess not," he said like a kid who had been given socks for Christmas.

The doctor sat silently watching us go back and forth like a tennis match. Once we stopped talking, he asked, "What would my duties be?"

"Pretty simple. Treat me, Billy, and anyone else who might be injured."

"I'm going to assume you have a place nearby designated for treatment."

I got up and started for the door.

"I'll show you."

The doctor rose and followed along, with Billy bringing up the rear. We walked down the hall to the infirmary. I stepped inside and waited by the door, leaving the doctor lead the way inside to look at the equipment. He took a long, slow lap around the room, picking up an instrument here, and opening a drawer there. Finally, he stepped over to me.

"I'll need some more equipment," he said.

"Make me a list, I'll get it."

"I see you already have blood on hand, I assume it's yours and his."

"Correct."

"Very astute of you to plan ahead like that."

"Thanks, is there anything else you'd need?"

"An assistant for if I'm unavailable, or if I have a difficult procedure."

"This would be someone you trust?"

He nodded.

"Someone I could also trust to keep our secrets?"

He nodded again.

"Would this assistant be on call as well?"

"Of course?"

"How much would they need to be paid?"

"Two hundred and fifty thousand a year."

"Done."

I offered my hand and he shook it.

"Would you like to see the rest of the place?"

"I think that would be wise," he said.

I took him on a tour of the house with Billy following along behind us. At some point Billy lost interest and disappeared. When I was done, I offered the doctor to stay for lunch, but he declined. We discussed details and he left.

Billy reappeared soon after.

"Is he gone?" Billy said.

"Yes, he just left."

"Dangit, I wanted to see him off."

"Then why didn't you?" I said. "Where'd you go anyway?"

"Oh, I just got sidetracked," he said avoiding my eyes.

"Whatever, I've got to go order the doctor's list," I said, walking away leaving him standing there staring at the wall.

A short while later there was a knock at my office door. I glanced up and there stood Dolores.

"Hey, stranger," I said. "Long time, no see. How've you been?"

I motioned to the chair across the desk and she stepped in and sat.

"I'm good, how are you?"

"Just got back from vacation," I said with a smile.

"Say no more," she said returning the smile. "How's your sidekick?"

"He seems better."

"Does he?"

"Yes, why?"

Just then, Billy poked his head in the door.

"Hello," he said.

"Why hello, young man," Dolores said with a smile. "We haven't been properly introduced, I'm Dolores."

"Are you the one who saved our lives when Dell… " Billy said.

"I stepped in and bought some time for others to save you," she said.

"So, in other words, yes, she did save our lives," I said.

"Thank you very much," Billy said, stepping forward and offering his hand.

Dolores shook it.

"It was my pleasure, young man," she said smiling. "I wonder if I could bother you for a cup of tea."

"Sure thing," Billy beamed. "Anything for you."

As Billy turned and headed for the kitchen, Dolores waved her hand and the door silently blew closed.

"I came to speak to you about something that's been bothering me," she said, suddenly serious.

"Ok… "

She sighed and hesitated for a long moment.

"I'm not sure how much you know about banshees."

"Very little actually."

"We have a code. We're not supposed to inform anyone that we've had a vision about them until right before it happens."

"That seems a little… unhelpful."

She shrugged.

"It is what it is, however, you've put me in a position where I feel I have to break that rule."

"Why?"

She paused for a moment, staring at the floor.

"No one has ever treated me like you have."

"I didn't mean to… "

"You don't understand," she said. "I've revealed my true identity to others, and every one of them has turned their back on me, except you."

I sat back in my chair, genuinely surprised.

"I don't know what to say."

She wiped her suddenly moist eyes.

"You accepted me as a friend, regardless of knowing what I truly am," she said. "Our friendship has been a gift."

"Has been?"

"I came to tell you you're in danger."

"It seems like I'm always in danger anymore," I said with a grin.

"This is different," she said without a trace of humor. "Someone close to you will betray you."

"How close?" I said leaning further back in my chair.

"Not me, you idiot."

She paused as Billy came in with the cup of tea.

"Here you go," he said.

She beamed at him.

"Thank you so much, young man, I wonder if you have any honey."

"I'll go check."

As soon as he left, she turned back to me and her face was set in stone. She nodded her head in the direction of the door.

"What, I'm gonna get trapped in the doorway?"

"No," she said slamming her teacup onto the desk. "He will betray you."

"Who, Billy?" I said, laughing. "He's the most honest, innocent soul I've ever met. That boy couldn't hurt a fly. Which makes me rethink why he's helping me hunt cryptids."

"I've had a vision," she said. "I saw you in mortal danger at his hands."

"Billy attacked me?"

"Attacked... and killed."

"Billy killed me?"

"The vision becomes hazy at that point, but it seemed so."

I sat back in my chair, mouth wide open.

"How many of your visions haven't come true?"

She shook her head solemnly.

"But wait, the vision you had about Billy dying that brought you here to save us."

"It came true."

"What do you mean it came true, he's still alive."

"But he did die, in the hospital."

I opened my mouth to deny it, but she was right. The doctor said Billy died and they had to resuscitate him.

Just then, Billy returned with the honey.

"Thank you so much," she said, smiling.

Billy's smile faded when he saw me.

"Everything alright, boss?" Billy said.

I scrutinized the face of the person I thought I trusted and shook myself mentally.

"Yeah, it's all good."

"I've given him some distressing news about someone close to him," Dolores said.

"Oh, I'm sorry, boss, I hope everything turns out ok," Billy said.

I stared into his eyes and all I saw was innocence.

"I hope so too," I said.

Chapter 10

I drove to the ranger station the following morning, Dolores' words still echoing in my mind.

'He will betray you.'

Out of all the impossible things I'd experienced over the last several months, Billy betraying me seemed the most unbelievable. It just went against everything I knew about him.

But what did I really know about him?

I'd never even met his parents. Of course, I'm his employer, not his fiancée. There was no reason for me to meet or ask about his parents. And let's not forget, I originally hired him as little more than a human shield in case one of these critters was about to get a hold of me.

Wow, was I really that cold and arrogant? No wonder Billy's going to turn on me.

But he's not. He can't. It's not in his makeup. He could no more turn on me than he could sprout wings and fly to the moon. Dolores must've gotten confused.

My thoughts were interrupted when the ranger station came into view. I sighed heavily wondering what stupidity would pour out of this building today.

I walked in and all eyes fell on me with what I could only describe as terror. I got a cup of coffee and headed to Dell's former office which was technically now my office until the Ranger's service decided to replace me.

As I turned the corner, I saw Jeff sitting at my desk, facing the window with his feet propped up on the windowsill. I listened to his side of the conversation.

"That's right," he said into the phone. "I'm the boss now."

…

"That clown they put in charge? He has no idea of how to run a ranger's station."

…

"I'm telling you, I'd be surprised if he ever has the guts to show his face around here anymore."

…

"Dell was a jerk, but he was a thousand times better than this buttwipe."

…

I stood there quietly listening as I sipped my coffee.

"I might just give him a call and tell him he's fired."

…

"I just wish he was here right now so I could tell him… "

He stopped talking as he turned and saw me standing there.

"I gotta go."

He hung up the phone and before he could say a word, I whipped out my Taser and squeezed the trigger. The hooks hit him in the leg and chest. He twitched like a fish as a strange sound that was half scream and half whimper emerged from him.

"Stop that!" Nancy yelled from behind me.

I whipped around on her as the five-second charge ended and Jeff's body settled into the chair.

"Stop what," I said, looking at the Taser. "You mean this?"

I squeezed the trigger, sending another fifty-thousand volts of electricity surging into Jeff's body.

"Yes, that, stop it," she said.

"Wait, you said, yes?" I said as the five-second charge ended. "Ok, yes."

I squeezed the trigger again.

Jeff's body once again went into convulsions.

Nancy tried to grab the Taser from me, but I pulled back making her hands connect with the wires and sending shocks racing through her body.

She collapsed to the floor as the taser ran out of charge.

I ejected the cartridge, then went over to the charging station and loaded up with a new battery and cartridge.

I dumped Jeff's immobile body out of my chair and left him lying there, face down with his butt in the air, unable to move.

I turned toward the rest of the rangers.

"So, what else has been going on in my absence?"

Ron and Sharon glanced at each other.

"Nothing," Ron said.

I put the Taser back in its holster and regarded at them.

"Aren't you supposed to be out patrolling or something?"

They both nearly fell over each other trying to get out the door.

Nancy stirred and got up to the kneeling position, clawing the edge of my desk to steady herself.

"You've just committed a felony, attacking two federal officers," she said.

I pulled the Taser out of its holster and put the red aiming dot right on her chest.

"Nothing to stop me from committing another then is there?"

"Please don't," she pleaded.

"What are the words I'm looking for?"

She thought for a moment.

"I won't tell anyone."

"Look at that," I said. "And I didn't even need to prompt you. You do have a brain after all."

She straightened, glaring at me like she desperately wanted to say something, but I still had the Taser aimed at her.

"If there's nothing else, sir, I should go out on my patrol route."

"Dismissed," I said holstering the Taser.

For just an instant she seemed like she wanted to come at me, but I kept my hand on the taser.

She left the room and I propped my feet on Jeff's butt which was frozen in the air as I sipped my coffee.

"I just might like this job after all," I said, watching birds fly past the window.

It took a few minutes for him to start moaning and eventually fall over onto his side. His eyes fluttered open and he wiped the drool from his mouth as he rolled over to the sitting position.

"So, who were you talking to on the phone?" I said.

He glared at me silently.

I moved my hand toward the Taser.

"My wife!" he said, throwing both arms in front of his face as if that would block the Taser.

"Oh my God, someone actually agreed to marry you?" I said, incredulous. "What kind of blackmail did that take?"

His eyes burned with rage, but he kept them focused on the holster.

"So, here's what you're gonna do," I said. "Call your wife back and tell her you're an idiot. Not that she doesn't already know that if she has more than two brain cells. Which could be questioned if she married you."

As he listened his eyes teetered back and forth between rage and confusion.

"Am I fired?" he said.

"Call your wife."

He picked up his phone off the floor and dialed.

"Hey, honey," he said.

...

"Yes, I know."

...

"I've got bad service here in the station. I must've dropped the call."

...

"I was just saying... " he glared at me and I raised an eyebrow. "That I'm an idiot."

...

"What do you mean, you knew that?"

I did my best to keep from laughing.

...

"You've known what for years?"

...

"Oh really?"

…

"Your signal's breaking up. I'm losing you again."

He hit the end call button, then sat brooding, refusing to look at me.

"Am I fired?"

I stared at him for a long moment, long enough to make him squirm.

"Of course… you're not fired."

He breathed a sigh of relief.

"I'm looking forward to target practice every morning when I get my coffee."

His eyes grew wide as he glanced from my eyes to the Taser and back again.

"You wouldn't."

My grin grew from ear to ear as I unholstered the Taser.

"Ok you would, you would, you would," he squealed covering his eyes with one arm and holding his hand out as if to block the electrical charge somehow.

I holstered the weapon and sat back in my chair.

"I think you have a route to patrol," I said, turning on the computer.

He peeked from under his arm and saw nothing pointed at him. Then he slowly rose and headed for the door.

"One more thing," I said just before he stepped through the doorway.

He paused but didn't look back.

"Who's the greatest boss in the world?" I said.

He tensed up for a moment, his hands formed into fists, then he relaxed, and his shoulders slumped.

"You are," he said.

"Damn straight. Don't forget it."

He trudged to the door and out of the station.

I turned to the window and watched him go. I could already see him mumbling.

'Yep,' I thought, sipping on my coffee. 'I'm definitely going to enjoy this job.'

I turned on the computer and started searching through the federal database for Billy's name. A few minutes later, nothing came up. He wasn't hiding anything, at least nothing he'd gotten in trouble for.

I called the local high school and talked to the principal, pretending to be an employer interested in hiring Billy. The principal had nothing but glowing remarks to say about him. He had been in the top half of his class, never got in trouble, but never really excelled at anything. Just one of those kids who flew under the radar and was a solid citizen.

I thanked her and hung up the phone more confused than ever. If Billy had some dark past, I could see where there might be a chance of betrayal. But there was nothing. The kid was as clean as a baby's behind.

I opened my phone and called Dolores.

"Hello?" she said on the third ring.

"I'm just wondering how that kid could betray me."

"Not much for small talk today, are you?"

"I'm serious, this is bothering me. I keep wanting to say you're wrong."

"I want the same thing, believe me, but I saw it."

"Can you tell me the vision?"

She sighed heavily.

"I'm not supposed to… "

"But you will," I said, in a voice that wasn't threatening or pleading, just matter-of-fact.

There was silence on the line for a long moment.

"It was dark, you were outside, somewhere in the forest," she said. "Billy was beside you looking terrified. It appeared as if you two were searching for someone or something."

"Like a cryptid?"

"Possibly, but something was wrong. You seemed more worried than usual. You weren't talking or acting like your usual self."

"Charming?"

"Incorrigible."

"Nice," I said sarcastically.

"Whatever it was, you both seemed to think you were getting close, and then something happened."

"What? What happened?"

She paused for a moment as if unsure if she should continue.

"The moon rose."

"Yeah, so?"

"And Billy changed… "

I leaned back in my chair, not realizing I had been leaning forward, hanging on her every word.

"He changed into what?"

"I think you know."

I flashed back to when we were fighting Dell. He tore Billy nearly to pieces with his claws… and fangs.

"He couldn't," I said, wishing I believed it.

Dolores didn't say a word.

"He couldn't," I said a little more forcefully.

"I'm sorry," she said.

I sat staring at the wall, envisioning my assistant, no, my friend, tear me to pieces in the middle of the woods.

"What do I do?" I said quietly, almost a whisper.

"I don't know," she said. "I think things are already in motion."

"But if he was, I don't know the term, infected, I guess, wouldn't he be showing some signs, like peeing in the corner or carrying the paper in each morning in his mouth?"

"There are signs you can look for," she said.

"Like what?" I said, desperately looking through the desk drawer for pen and paper.

"Insomnia," she said. "Headaches, and flu-like symptoms."

"That's it?" I said, hoping for something more specific.

"As far as I know."

"How long until he… "

"Fully turns? Anywhere between one and three months."

My mind did some quick calculations.

"It's been eighteen days since he was attacked," I said.

"Has he shown any symptoms?"

"Not that I've noticed," I said, thinking back over the last two weeks.

"You're going to have to keep a close eye on him."

"And then what? Is there any cure?"

"None that I'm aware of, except a silver bullet."

"Not happening," I said. "It's not his fault."

"Is that what you'd like me to put on your tombstone?"

"Stop that! We haven't even established that he's been infected."

"I have."

"Ok, but I'd like something more concrete than your vision, no offense."

"None taken."

There was a heavy silence on both ends of the phone.

"What are you going to do?" she asked.

"I'm not sure," I said. "Something unorthodox."

"Of that, I have no doubt. Take care."

The line disconnected.

I stared at the computer, not really looking at the screen but through it, as my thoughts raced.

An alert flashed up on the screen. Hikers had reported something strange in the woods. I read the report and immediately jumped in my truck.

I drove home like a bat out of hell, ran through my destroyed front door and into my office. I opened the book I'd liberated from Dell's office and flipped through pages until I found what I was looking for.

"Bil... " I started to yell but he was already standing in the doorway.

I jumped a little, my hip sending me a painful reminder that it wasn't completely healed.

"Yeah, boss?" he said.

"Stop doing that."

"Doing what?"

"Sneaking up on me."

"Sorry, boss," he said, but I noticed a slight grin.

"Whatever, it looks like we've got a cryptid," I said, showing him the file in the book.

"That looks like a good one to get us back on track," he said, smiling.

"Well, what are you waiting for?" I said, showing him the list of useful items to defeat this cryptid that was listed in the book.

"On my way," he said turning and heading toward the armory.

I stayed in the office and called Marie.

"I need some repairs on the house," I said.

"Already?"

"An uninvited guest did some extreme remodeling."

"Alright, I'll have a work crew there in two days."

"I also wanted to discuss something with you face to face."

"You're not going to pull a gun on me again, are you?"

"Not this time," I said. "I just need to ask you a question."

"And you can't do that over the phone?"

I glanced up as Billy returned and gave me a thumbs up.

"Most certainly not," I said returning his gesture.

"Alright, I'll be there tomorrow," she said. "We can discuss renovations and whatever your mystery topic is."

"Thanks, I'll see you then."

I hung up the phone and rose, heading for the door.

"Who was that?"

"Marie, my assistant."

"I thought I was your assistant," he said as we headed for the front door.

"She's my assistant who makes me money."

"I thought I helped you make money."

"It's ok, son," I said sarcastically. "I love you just as much as your sister."

"What?" he said, looking at me like I had sprouted a second head.

"It was a joke."

He still looked like a dog that had heard a strange sound.

"Never mind," I said, starting the truck and heading down the driveway.

We drove for about an hour, well outside of our territory, but then I didn't really have a territory. I considered stopping in at the local sheriff station and offering a bribe to save time, but this remote there was no telling if they would even respond to a cryptid sighting.

The closer we got to where the report said the creature was, the more I wished I had stopped off at Dolores' house and convinced her to go along for the ride.

If Billy really was a werewolf, it would be nice to have some backup.

'If Billy really was a werewolf'. I couldn't believe I was really having that thought. If she hadn't been so deadly serious, I would've thought this was Dolores playing a prank on me. But I knew that look when she sat across from me in my office and first told me. She wasn't playing.

"You ok over there, boss?" Billy said, dragging me out of my thoughts and into the present.

"Yeah, sure, why?"

"You're just quieter than usual. Something up?"

"No, I'm fine," I lied. "Just lost in thought. How have you been feeling?"

"A-ok."

I gave him the look.

"Well, I mean I'm still having some aches and pains, but that's natural."

"After what we've been through, aches and pains are just confirmation that we're still alive."

"I guess," he said. "Oh, and I have been having a little trouble sleeping lately."

My spine froze.

"You have insomnia?" I said slowly.

"It's not too bad. I take some sleeping pills and they help."

"Must be from all the injuries," I said hopefully.

"I'm sure, plus all the people in the house."

"All what people? You mean the workers?"

"I don't know who they are, but they come into my room sometimes without knocking."

"The workers went home last week," I said. "There hasn't been anyone in the house but you and me since the doctor left the other day."

He turned pale.

"Then we might wanna get the security system checked because someone was in my room talking to me last night."

Now it was me turning pale.

"Describe them."

"It was an old lady," he said. "I've seen her around the house ever since I came back from the hospital. I just figured she was a housekeeper or something."

"Have you seen anything else?" I said quietly.

"A few others here and there, but mostly she's the one that talks to me."

"What did she say?"

"She asked general questions, what're we doing there? How long have we been there? When are we leaving? She didn't talk about herself much. I figured she was having trouble sleeping too and just wanted to talk to someone."

I didn't realize I had been staring at him the whole time until I heard the truck horn blaring. My head snapped up and I was in the wrong lane with a big rig bearing down on me. I swerved back into my own lane just in time as he gave me the finger and laid on the horn.

I pulled over to the berm and put the truck in park.

Billy was white-knuckling the 'oh shit' handle by his door.

"You ok, boss?" he said.

I thought about the conversation we'd been having, and what we were doing here, chasing another dangerous cryptid in less than ideal shape. I thought about the fact that I nearly made Dolores' prediction moot by killing us both in a car wreck. But mostly I thought about the potential ticking time bomb that was sitting in the seat next to me, wearing a look of concern, asking me if I was ok.

"Sure," I said, putting the truck back in gear and pulling onto the road. "I'm super."

We didn't talk the rest of the way.

We pulled into the park and I went straight to the ranger's station. I told them I had seen the report about the missing hikers and wanted to help if I could.

The head ranger said he appreciated it and showed me a map of where they were currently searching. I thanked him and headed in that general direction.

The sun was hanging low in the sky by the time we parked and got out to load up for our search.

"I'm starving," Billy said. "I wish we would've stopped somewhere to grab a bite."

I flinched when he said bite.

"There's plenty of granola bars and bottled water in the back," I said. "Just make sure to leave enough room in your pack for the equipment we need."

We loaded up our packs. I shook my head when I noticed quite a few granola bars going into his. We got the rest of our equipment loaded and then strapped on our utility belts, which included a Taser, tranq gun, and pistol for each of us, with plenty of extra rounds.

I hesitated seeing him armed as well as me. The whole, 'he will betray you' still weighing heavily on me. You would think I would avoid taking him with me in dangerous situations if I wasn't sure I could trust him. But I didn't have anyone else except

Dolores, and I had no desire to drag her through the forest.

We started easy, walking down the trail where the hikers had been seen last. The heavy backpack wasn't doing my healing hip any good. I noticed Billy was taking it slow too. For a moment I thought about turning around and heading back home, retiring, and moving as far away from Billy as possible.

But instead, I kept trudging down the trail with Billy right behind me.

The sun had set and taken most of the light with it. We pulled out our flashlights and continued down the path. The sounds of the woodland creatures all around comforted me. They were interrupted by the sound of granola wrappers being opened one at a time in continuous succession.

I stopped and turned, shining the light in his face.

"Are you nearly done?" I said as he munched on a bar.

"I told you I was hungry," he said.

I stopped dead. Behind him in the woods was a creature. It stood taller than a man and there were wings on its back. They were big and almost reminded me of a butterfly. No, not a butterfly, a moth. Its eyes glowed red as it hovered there staring at us.

"Don't move," I tried to say moving my mouth as little as possible. "Slowly take your tranq gun out and hold it at your side."

"What's going on?" he said moving his mouth as little as possible.

"Our target is right behind you."

He started shaking.

"Stop it!" I whisper shouted through gritted teeth. "We've got this, just keep calm, and let's take it down."

He took out his gun as told and let it hang near his leg. The creature seemed to notice and hovered away a few feet. I reached for my gun and it disappeared.

"Dammit!" I said.

"What?"

"It's gone."

He slowly turned and scanned back where the creature had been.

"Where was it?" he said.

I pointed to the spot.

"I see something," he said.

"See what?"

"I don't know, like an outline of a person, hovering above the ground."

I squinted my eyes and scouted the spot.

"I don't see anything."

He started walking toward it as if he hadn't heard me. It was almost like he was in a trance. I followed along behind him, shining the light around to make sure it didn't show up unexpectedly.

He stopped so suddenly that I nearly ran into him.

"What's wrong?" I said.

He turned toward me, startled as if he'd forgotten I was there.

"He was here," he said pointing at empty air.

I shone my light at the spot he was pointing at but saw nothing.

"You don't need the light," he said in a strange voice. "I can see the glow of his outline."

All I saw was empty air.

"You can see its outline?"

"Right here," he said, pointing.

"I can't see it."

He scanned around, his eyes seeming unfocused.

"He's still here."

I turned, flashing the light all around, but didn't see anything. More disturbing, I didn't hear anything. The forest had gone deathly silent.

"I don't like this," I said.

He reached over and turned off my light.

"Let me see if I can find him."

The forest went dark as pitch without the flashlight. I had a hard time seeing Billy standing right next to me, let alone looking around for a cryptid that had disappeared and could be creeping up on us at any moment.

"There," I heard beside me, making me jump.

"Where? I can't see anything."

I turned on the light and panned around.

"Right there," Billy said pointing off to my left.

I shone the light where he was pointing and sure enough, I could see the faint outline of the creature hovering there.

"How did you… ?"

"I told you I could see his outline glowing."

"O… k… then how do we get him if we can't get close enough?"

"Let me try."

"Try what?"

He turned toward me with I look I'd never seen.

"Just let me try."

The intensity of his words surprised me so much I nearly took a step back.

"Ok, go ahead and try," I said, gesturing toward the creature who still hovered there watching us.

He started toward the creature, and I followed along at a respectful distance. I'd pulled out my tranq gun and tried to hide it behind my leg.

Billy walked toward it, his flashlight was off, and yet he didn't stumble once. It was as if something was guiding him. Meanwhile, I was tripping over branches even with the light. He stopped and turned toward me, putting his finger to his lips and telling me to stop making noise.

The snot-nosed little punk.

For the good of the mission, I stopped, but I was fuming. How dare he do better than me. It was like we had switched places. He was the experienced ranger, and I was the clumsy kid.

I stood still and quietly flicked off the safety on my tranq gun. He must've heard it somehow because he turned back toward me and slowly shook his head.

Oh, we were gonna have a serious conversation about this when we got back.

He approached the creature and to my great surprise, it didn't move. He reached out his hand toward it and it hovered down to ground level. It stepped toward him and put its hand out matching Billy's gesture. Their hands were just about to touch when the creature screamed.

Billy jumped back as it thrashed around falling to the ground in convulsions before laying still.

I stepped up beside Billy and admired my handiwork, pulling the tranq dart out of the creature's side.

"Not a bad shot if I do say so myself,' I said.

Billy's eyes burned with rage.

"Why did you do that?" he said.

"Do what?"

"Shoot him."

"That's what we came here to do," I said looking at him incredulously.

He stepped toward me, looking every bit like he wanted to take a swing at me. His eyes burned with rage. Then suddenly, as if someone had flicked a switch, he stopped and stared at me. Then he shook his head violently as if trying to shake out the cobwebs and walked away toward the trail.

"Where are you going?" I called after him, but he refused to turn or say anything.

I shrugged and called The Man.

Ten minutes later, his soldiers were carrying the creature out of the forest to the clearing where their helicopter had landed.

"Good work," The Man said, shaking my hand.

"I can't take all the credit; Billy distracted it so I could take my shot.

He scanned around.

"Where is he?"

"I don't know, he took off down the trail after I shot it."

"Why?"

"He was doing some weird thing with the creature. It was like he was connected to it somehow."

"How's he been feeling?"

"Healing, just like me," I said. "Other than that, the same old Billy."

"Except for tonight."

"Except for tonight," I agreed.

He stared at me, looking very serious.

"I'd like to take him with me and do some tests."

"No sale," I said. "He's doing fine. This creature just got to him. Maybe he had a butterfly collection as a kid."

"You do remember he was bit by a werewolf?"

"Really," I said sarcastically. "I had no idea. It must've been when I was fighting for my life."

"Alright, let's not get back into that again. I'm just saying you should be very careful."

"Thanks, Dad, I'll make sure to fill the car up before I bring it home."

"Smartass," he said without a hint of a grin.

"Seriously, I appreciate the concern, but Billy's fine."

He grunted, then turned and headed for the helicopter.

I watched as they flew away into the night. I should've asked for a lift to my truck, but I didn't need to answer any more awkward questions.

Why didn't I tell him about Dolores' vision?

Because he would've taken Billy right then no matter how much I protested. I still wanted to protect the kid, even though he might hideously tear me to pieces.

Perhaps I should rethink telling The Man.

I trudged along the trail seeing all kinds of glowing eyes staring at me as I went.

"Not tonight," I said to the eyes. "I'm tired and I already caught my quota."

The eyes didn't go away but didn't get any closer either.

When I got to the truck, Billy was leaning against it. I unlocked the doors and we both got in without a word.

I drove back in silence, concentrating on the road while he concentrated on staring out the window and brooding.

We were almost home when he finally spoke.

"Why did you do that?" he said.

"Do what?"

"Shoot him and turn him over like some animal."

"It is an animal," I said. "That's what we do. That's literally the entire reason we were there."

"He."

"What?"

"He was a male of his species."

"How do you know that?"

"Never mind."

"No, you started this, tell me, how did you know?"

He sighed.

"Because he told me."

"What?"

"I can't explain it, ok. It was just a feeling I got when I was looking for him."

"You got a feeling that this thing was talking to you?"

"I knew you wouldn't understand," he said, turning back toward his window.

I drove the last few miles in silence. When we got there, he got out of the truck and went inside.

I sat there for a moment, feeling every bit like the father of a teenager who'd just made the 'you don't understand me' speech.

I never signed up for this. I just wanted to make some money and have someone else around when things went bad.

I dragged myself inside, feeling more tired than I had in a long time. I stepped through the opening that used to be a door only to find Billy standing near the grandfather clock, facing the wall, and talking.

"He doesn't understand like you do," he said to the air. "I just can't talk to… "

He stopped and glared at me, then turned back to the empty wall and said, "We'll talk later."

He walked away, heading up the steps.

"I thought you said you were hungry," I called after him.

"Lost my appetite."

He disappeared down the hallway toward the bedrooms as I approached the empty spot where he had been standing. For some reason, I felt a chill but couldn't find anything he could be talking to. It was literally an empty section of wall.

I shook my head and went to the kitchen to grab a snack, then up to my room. When I passed Billy's doorway, I could hear him talking to someone. I

didn't bother to ask any more questions. I was just too
tired to deal with it.

Chapter 11

You've heard the expression it was raining cats and dogs, well as soon as we got back, the sky opened up and dumped everything on us. It was raining lions and wolves. I seriously started to think about building an ark after day two when it hadn't let up.

I called the ranger station and told Jeff he could be in charge of rescuing anyone who was dumb enough to be out in this kind of weather while I sat at home in front of a fire watching, 'Singing in the rain'.

For some reason, he sounded less than enthused about his assignment.

I sat in front of a fire, with my laptop. I'd decided to do a case file on each of the cryptids I'd caught. I was looking up this last one by description.

"He's a Mothman," Billy said in my ear.

I nearly jumped out of my skin, just barely keeping the laptop from crashing to the floor.

"Why do you keep sneaking up on me like that?" I said, trying to get comfortable again.

"Sorry," he said, not looking like he meant it.

"How do you know what that thing was anyway?"

"I'll tell you, but you won't believe me."

"After all the strange things we've seen, I highly doubt that."

"Ok, he told me his name and what people called him."

I stared at him.

"I don't believe it."

"Told you."

"How did it tell you? I didn't hear it say anything."

"You won't believe me."

"Are we doing this again? Just tell me."

"I heard him inside my mind."

My mouth dropped open, but I didn't make a sound.

"Go ahead," Billy sighed. "You can say it."

"I don't believe it."

"You know, you seem to have a hard time believing things for someone who's seen so much unbelievable stuff."

"Who are you, my therapist now?"

He shrugged.

"Do I get a pay raise?"

"No."

"Then I'm not your therapist."

For a long moment neither of us spoke, we just sat and listened to the rain pounding against the windows. I wondered if they would hold up against such a tempest.

Movement caught my attention and brought me back to the moment as I saw Billy shake his head. It wasn't much of a movement, but it was enough. I watched him out of the corner of my eye, but he wasn't looking at me. He was looking beside me at the empty couch as if someone was sitting there.

For the longest time, I saw him having this strange lip-moving, silent conversation with the air beside me on the couch. It would've been comical if it wasn't so weird. I was convinced he was playing a prank on me and wanted me to react so he could say he got me.

But some nagging feeling told me it wasn't that.

I decided to pull an end around and told him I was going to bed. He said goodnight and I took my laptop up to my bedroom.

As I walked up the steps, I saw his silent conversation with the empty couch become more animated. He never once glanced back to see if I was watching him.

I closed the door to my bedroom and started for the desk, then paused and locked the door. It seemed such an odd thing to do in the safety of my own home, but with Billy acting so weird, I figured better safe than sorry.

I can't believe I just thought that. I must be getting old.

I sat my laptop on the desk and started out on a new mission, closing my cryptid file after entering the name Mothman.

Accessing the interior cameras, I began going back over footage, focusing on Billy's comings and goings. He walked backward at incredible speed as I rewound the footage. It was comical to watch, especially when he talked. I never realized how much of an animated talker he was.

Suddenly I slowed the recording and resumed it forward at normal speed. He had stopped by the grandfather clock and was standing there for a good ten minutes just staring at the wall. No, he wasn't just staring, he was talking to the wall. Just like I'd seen him do the other day.

Watching as he held his conversation, he suddenly became startled and looked away from the wall, just as I walked through. He followed along with me but glanced back at the wall and shrugged like he was apologizing for walking away.

I picked up my phone and called Marie.

"Hello?" she said sounding very asleep.

"The cameras you installed, do they have any other capabilities than just normal recording?"

"What… time… is… it… ?"

"I don't know, time doesn't really have much meaning for me anymore."

"It's one in the morning."

"Ok, then you answered your own question."

"I was asleep."

"Really, what're you wearing?"

"Ha ha, very funny," she said. "I'm wearing a sexual harassment lawsuit."

"Oh, sounds kinky, is it see-through?"

"What do you want?" she said louder and more slurry.

"I told you what I want. I want to know if the cameras have any other modes."

"I think so. On the bottom right, there should be three dots, click on them."

"Ok, it says options, and then it says, oh, cool, other camera modes. Thanks."

"No problem," she slurred right before the line went dead.

I rewound the video to where Billy was talking to the wall and paused the video. I cycled through the camera options one at a time, not noticing much except the screen changing colors until suddenly I froze.

There on the screen in psychedelic colors was what seemed like a person standing in front of Billy, having a conversation with him. I leaned back in the chair feeling the blood drain from my face as this invisible being chit-chatted with my assistant, confidant, and dare I say it, friend.

The most chilling part of the scene was that he'd hidden it from me. He didn't tell me he was seeing people that I couldn't see. Or did he? Thinking back, I remembered times he said there were people in the house and I just explained it away as being work crews or whatever. I hadn't listened to him. Could be that's why he chose not to pursue it.

And then I thought back to this evening when he was talking to the couch. That wasn't an innocent miscommunication, he was telling this being not to try to communicate with me. He was deliberately hiding the truth from me.

I pressed a button on my phone and made another call.

"This better be important," The Man said, as heard explosions in the background. "No, the left side, cover the left side."

Automatic rifle fire opened up and I heard what could only be described as a roar.

"It's breaking through! Full lethal authorized!" The Man said.

"Are you in danger?" he said, focusing back on me.

"No, I just need to ask a question, but you're busy, so I'll let you... "

"Go ahead and ask," he said as another explosion rattled the speaker in my phone.

"Can you catch a ghost?"

The line was silent with the exception of rifle fire in the background followed by another roar.

"Let me get back to you," he said, then disconnected the line.

I stared at the phone and made a mental decision to never question him again about showing up on time.

Leaning back in my chair, I stared at the image frozen on my laptop of the entity having a conversation with Billy.

The rain pounded the windows, but I barely heard it. My mind was running in circles. After a while of staring at the screen, I was still no closer to knowing what to do.

Closing the laptop, I went to bed. But sleep didn't come easy.

***

Hours later I woke to the buzzing of my phone. I swung at it and knocked it to the floor, then grumbled and fell out of bed trying to retrieve it.

"Yeah," I said when I finally got a hold of it.

"It sounds like I'm disturbing you now," The Man said.

"Nope, just sleeping," I said. "Nothing like what you were going through during the last call.

"Oh, that? That was a minor concern, nothing we couldn't handle."

'Damn,' I thought. 'That was minor?'

"Anyways, to answer your question, yes and no."

"Well, that's as clear as mud."

"Yes, we can catch a ghost, but there have to be some specific circumstances."

"Ok, well I have pictures on my laptop, if I send you those, will it help you decide?"

"Go ahead and send them," he said. "We'll analyze the situation and see what can be done."

"Understood, chief."

"In the meantime, go back to bed."

"Yes, sir," I said with a mock salute even though I knew he couldn't see it.

The line disconnected.

Sleep wasn't happening. The excitement was too much. I went through more video, isolating and sending a copy of every instance of the ghost that I saw. Most of them seemed to center around Billy. There were very few occurrences of the ghost appearing alone.

I couldn't believe I was gathering physical evidence of not only a ghost's existence but its habits and movements. Yet another thing I never thought I'd be doing just a few months ago.

Finishing up the package, I sent it off to The Man, then finally crawled back in bed and closed my eyes.

***

"Hey, baby, do you want to go again?" came a lovely feminine voice in my ear.

"Sure," I said rolling over and looking up at a fully dressed and smiling Marie.

"If we're gonna go again, you'll need to remove those clothes."

"I think you know I was joking."

"Not cool," I said yawning and stretching. "So to what do I owe the honor of this breaking and entering?"

"I only entered," she said holding up a key card.

"Did I give you that?"

"I may or may not have made my own copy in case I needed access to any room in the house."

"Including my bedroom?" I said making my eyebrows go up and down.

"Don't flatter yourself," she said. "I was just getting you back. You woke me up, now it's your turn."

"You didn't read that little clause in your contract that says anyone entering my bedroom is subject to extreme lovin'?"

"What contract?"

"The one I just wrote in my head."

"Yeah, I don't think so," she said. "Whenever you're ready to talk to me about your super secret subject, come down to the office."

I reached out and grabbed her hand.

"You have three seconds to let me go," she said.

"Ok, sorry," I said, releasing her. "I just can't be sure about the office anymore."

Her serious expression turned curious.

"What's wrong with the office?"

"It's not what, it's who."

She shook her head.

"It's too early in the morning for this. Please start making sense."

"I need you to restrict Billy's access to one room."

"The kid? Why?"

I shook my head.

"It's a long story, I just need you to do it."

"O… K… " she said slowly backing toward the door.

She turned to leave then stopped.

"You mean you want him to only have access to one room?"

"What? No."

"Well, think about what you said. I need you to restrict Billy's access to one room."

My mouth fell open as I realized she was right.

"Ok, I need to have one room that I can access, and Billy can't. Is that better?"

"It's clearer, even if I have no idea why."

"It needs to be somewhere out of the way. Some room he barely ever uses."

"I'll go over some video and see which room is best."

She turned and left.

I pulled the blanket over my head when I heard a knock at the door.

"Didn't I make it clear?" I said, not wanting to get up.

Billy opened the door and stepped in.

"Make what clear?"

"Sorry, I was talking to Marie."

He glanced around.

"Do you see her in the room?"

"She went down to the office, smartass."

"Ok, I'll go talk to her."

"You do that," I said, rolling over and burying my head in my pillow.

A few hours later I woke up refreshed but annoyed. I went downstairs to see what kind of damage had been done in my absence. As I walked into the office, Billy's head whipped around, and he stared at me.

"I guess I'll get going," he said to Marie who was sitting at my computer looking busy.

"Alright, I'll talk to you later," she said as Billy got up and pushed past me.

"What was that about?" I said sitting in the chair he had just vacated.

She sighed and sat back in the chair.

"You need to have a talk with him," she said. "I've been trying to get him out of this office so I can do what you asked, but he wouldn't stop talking."

"You're an attractive woman and his raging teenage hormones appear to have noticed."

"Ha ha, very funny," she said. "All he wanted to talk about was you."

"Me?"

"He's not very happy with you. Especially after this whole Mothman thing."

I shrugged.

"Eh, he'll get over it."

She leaned forward on the desk and steepled her fingers.

"I'm not so sure."

"I'll buy him a truck to destroy and try to teach him to drive again."

"What?"

"Long story, did you get done what I asked?"

"It took a while. Having company was distracting, but I was able to find a room he's visited only once."

She turned the monitor so I could see and I began laughing as soon as I realized which room it was.

"What's funny?"

"That's the room… " I said, then stopped when I saw her expectant eyes. "He's afraid of that room."

"Why?"

"Another long story."

"Nope, stop stonewalling me. What happened in that room?"

I sighed.

"We got chased in there by… a dangerous creature and were only able to escape due to dumb luck."

"That's it?"

"For now."

Her eyes bored into mine.

"When are you going to stop keeping secrets from me?"

"I don't know, on our tenth wedding anniversary?"

She snorted and turned the screen back to her.

"In your dreams."

I heard a throat clear and whipped around to see The Man standing there in the doorway.

"Am I interrupting?" he said.

"No," Marie said. "I was just gathering more evidence for my sexual harassment lawsuit."

She stood and marched toward the door.

"Will that be all, sir?" she said, stopping just short of the door and turning back towards me.

"No ma'am," I said.

She turned and walked past The Man, giving him a slight nod.

"You certainly like to keep things lively, don't you?" he said stepping in and looking for an available chair.

I motioned him to the one on the other side of my desk that Marie had just left.

"Are you sure?"

"You've paid for all of this, you might as well enjoy the big chair," I said.

"No, you've paid for it, with all your hard work."

He sat in the chair and settled in.

"This is nice, I might have to get one of these for my office."

"Only the best," I said. "So, what can I do for you? I doubt this is a social call."

"I brought the equipment you wanted."

I stared at him blankly.

"To catch the ghost," he said.

"Oh, right. How long do you think before it's up and running?"

He glanced at his watch.

"I'd say about nine minutes."

"What?"

"My men are installing it as we speak."

"Wow, do you ever take a vacation?"

"I did… once."

I eyed him expectantly, waiting for him to continue, but of course, he didn't.

"So, how's Billy?" he said.

"He's doing just fine," I said. "The picture of health."

"Um-hmm," he said, his eyes boring into mine.

"Did I hear my name?" Billy said from the doorway.

"Yes, young man," The Man said. "I was asking how you've been feeling since you left the hospital."

"Pretty good," he said as I shot The Man a triumphant look. "Except for my headaches, trouble sleeping, oh, and I've been feeling like I may have caught a cold or something."

The Man shot me a look that wasn't triumphant or gloating, it was dripping with concern.

"You should keep an eye on that," he said to Billy. "Complications from such an injury can be… severe."

"You think I should go back to the doctor?" Billy said.

"I'm sure you'll be fine," I said. "He's just being overly cautious."

"Oh, ok, why are you here anyway?" Billy said. "Usually, you grab whatever creature we have and fly away."

"I brought some special equipment for you two to capture… "

"… Our next cryptid," I said, cutting him off.

"You think it'll get inside?" Billy said.

"It's a difficult creature," I said. "Just want to be prepared in case something happens."

The Man sat watching us silently.

"Oh, ok, I guess better safe than sorry," Billy said. "Well, if you'll excuse me, I think I'm gonna go take some cold medicine and lay down."

He nodded to us then turned and left. The Man watched him go then turned his gaze to me.

"No," I said. "You're not taking him."

He silently stared at me.

"I said no."

His eyes bored into mine.

"I know what you're thinking that I might regret that decision."

His watch dinged.

"Looks like we're finished installing your traps," he said getting up. "Would you like to see how they work?"

I followed him out into the main hallway, and we stopped beside the grandfather clock. I scanned around but didn't see anything out of the ordinary.

"Where's all the equipment?"

"Hidden so the prey doesn't know it's there."

"So how will I know if I've caught one or not?" I said.

"The same way you knew it was there, watch the cameras."

"I guess I was expecting one of those shoebox-looking traps like Ghostbusters."

He turned and grinned at me.

"We have the real thing."

I opened my phone and switched to the internal security cameras, then clicked through to find an image of The Man and me standing near the grandfather clock. I switched it to the same spectrum I had used to see the ghost and then showed him the image. As he watched, suddenly his eyes grew wide.

"Watch out!" he said, pushing me back toward the far wall and diving to the floor beside me.

I was just about to ask him what his deal was when lights began to flash up and down the hall. There was a tremendous crashing sound as the grandfather clock fell to the floor. Streams of light flashed all around the spot where the clock had stood. I was confused at first, but then I saw an image appear. It was an old woman in an old-style dress, but she appeared to be in pain. Something held her immobile like she was being electrocuted. She shook as the electricity poured through her. Then suddenly she screamed.

It was unlike anything I'd ever heard before. It sounded like a chorus of screams in every octave and some that weren't humanly possible.

In the middle of this, Billy came rushing down the stairs. He saw what was happening and dove toward the woman.

"No!" he screamed as I tackled him before he could reach her.

"Let me go!" he screamed as he thrashed in my grip. "You're killing her!"

I didn't bother with the obvious argument that she was already dead, I just held on to keep him out of the explosion of light. His strength was surprising. It was all I could do to keep a hold of him as he clawed at the floor trying to reach her. He even managed to drag me along a few inches, and I outweighed him by a good fifty pounds.

Her scream ended as she started to fade. She glared at Billy with an expression that I would only call betrayal as she disappeared, and the lights stopped.

The room returned to normal lighting and smoke rose from the spot where the grandfather clock used to be.

The Man stepped over and picked up a small box that I hadn't noticed before. It was the size of a small shoebox.

"The real thing, huh?" I said, walking over and looking at the innocuous-looking metal container.

He shrugged. "It works for us."

Billy jumped up and ran at The Man, who dodged him with practiced ease, sending Billy sprawling on the floor. He sprang back up and rushed him again. I caught him in a bear hug and held him away from The Man.

"How could you?" Billy shrieked, spittle flying from his mouth. "She wasn't hurting anyone. She was my friend."

The Man stood silent in a ready stance, holding the box just out of Billy's reach.

Three men appeared out of nowhere and approached Billy, but The Man held up his hand freezing them in their tracks.

He managed to squirm his way out of my grasp and stood there breathing hard.

"Why can't you ever let things be?" he said, glaring daggers at me. "All I wanted was a friend to talk to, but no, you have to catch them and sell them off like pieces of meat. All for your damn money! Well, I'm done. I don't want any more of you or your selfish, self-righteous attitude. I quit!"

He turned and walked toward the door, the men glanced from him to The Man, silently asking for orders. I saw what was happening and stood between the men and Billy, shaking my head at The Man.

Billy stopped at the door and turned back.

"All you do is use people," he said to me. "It's no wonder you don't have any friends. You're gonna die alone and I hope I'm there to see it."

Then he stormed out the door.

I turned to The Man.

"Let him go," I said, then added. "Please."

His response was a curt nod, then a motion to his men. They filed out through the door, and I soon heard a helicopter engine start.

I looked around at my destroyed clock and hallway then sighed.

The Man stepped to the doorway and stopped.

"He's wrong," he said, turning back toward me.

"No, he's not," I said without looking.

A few minutes later I heard the helicopter fly away. I searched my phone and scrolled through the cameras until I found the one at the edge of the driveway. Billy was marching determinedly toward town. I watched as he disappeared out of range of the camera.

I sighed and walked to my office. It was so quiet I heard the echo of my footsteps as I walked down the destroyed hallway.

Plopping into my chair I turned on my computer and glanced over the icons I used the most and my eyes fell on the travel agency I frequented.

I wasn't feeling much like celebrating. I didn't book my usual trip. Instead, I went to the Paypal app and clicked on Billy's account, adding two hundred thousand dollars to it. In the space where it said, 'What's this for?' I typed in, 'For putting up with me.'

Chapter 12

I didn't wallow in self-pity. I immersed myself in it. My usual vacation plans went un-reserved. I added repairs to the hallway to Marie's list, with additional orders that I wasn't to be disturbed, and then went to bed. I don't remember much of what happened during the next few days. It consisted pretty much of eating and sleeping, with a side of self-loathing.

One day I woke to a soft knock on my door.

I grunted something rude and covered my head with my pillow. The next thing I knew the door opened.

"Are you deaf or just stupid? I said leave me alone!" I said.

I felt someone sit on the side of the bed. I shot up only to come face to face with Dolores.

"Good afternoon," she said smiling.

"What do you want?" I said, rolling away from her.

"I want you to stop torturing yourself."

"Why do you care?" I mumbled into a mouthful of pillow.

"Because I'm your friend."

"Really?" I said sitting up so quickly she flinched. "Because I was told I don't have any friends because I treat my friends like crap. I was told I was going to die alone."

"And do you believe that?"

I threw myself back onto the bed.

"It's true, isn't it? I treat everyone like crap."

"Of course it is, that's who you are."

I stopped and stared at her.

"Not everyone is meant to be a saint," she said. "In fact, if everyone were saints, there'd be no need for them."

"But I treat everyone close to me like garbage."

"You say you do, but I don't agree."

"But Billy… "

" …was upset," she said. "He wanted to hurt you the way he was hurting."

"Wait, how do you know what happened?"

"Marie and I had a nice little talk."

"But she wasn't there either."

Dolores lowered her eyes.

"I may have also called Thomas."

"Really? Wow, I didn't think you two were on speaking terms."

"He told me what happened, and he felt you might need someone to talk to."

"Surprising."

"Is it, really?" she said. "Thomas will never admit it, but I think he's grown quite fond of you."

"I'm spoken for."

"That's not what I meant, and you know it. Thomas isn't a man to give his trust lightly, but I feel like he would drop everything if you were in true peril."

"That didn't happen with Dell," I scoffed.

"No, it didn't. And I believe he regrets that. Besides didn't you two shake and make up about that?"

"Maybe," I said avoiding her eyes.

"Then stop bringing it up," she said with some force in her voice. "You don't want to treat people like crap then stop. Stop whining about things you've already resolved."

"Sure thing, Mom," I said covering my head with the blanket.

The cover flew off my bed with surprising strength, nearly taking me with it.

"What the... ?"

"Get your ass up and stop feeling sorry for yourself," she said staring at me with ferocity in her eyes.

I stood, towering over her by a good foot, but she didn't back down an inch.

"Good, now go get a shower, you smell like you've been wallowing in a pig sty."

I paused for a moment then stepped over to my dresser to grab some clean clothes and headed for the bathroom.

When I was done showering, shaving, and brushing my teeth, I felt much better. I stepped out of the bathroom with a flourish.

"Ta da!"

But no one was there.

I wondered for a moment if I had dreamed the whole thing or if she had some sort of power to invade peoples' thoughts.

I shrugged it off and headed downstairs to my office. Upon arriving I found Marie hard at work at my computer.

"Ah, there he is," she said. "It appears you've dragged yourself out of your pit of despair."

"Dolores tossed me a ladder," I said.

"I like her. We had a little chit-chat."

"About me?"

"No… well yes, but it wasn't… "

"Did you tell her how much you want me?" I said edging closer to my side of the desk.

She rolled her eyes.

"You're so juvenile."

"You didn't answer the question."

"No, I didn't tell her I had any feelings for you because I don't. Aside from wanting to kick your ass sometimes."

"Oo, sounds kinky."

"Ok, can you stop?"

"Alright," I said throwing up my hands in surrender.

"Thank you," she said continuing to work on the computer. "Why must you continually throw these sexual flirtations at me?"

"You need to look at yourself in the mirror more often."

"Why? Is something wrong?" she said feeling her hair to see if it was out of place.

"Nothing's wrong at all," I said leering at her.

"Stop it," she said, her cheeks turning red.

"Yes, Ma'am."

"So, down to business."

"Yes, it's about time you stopped fooling around," I said.

She fastened me with the, 'Really?' stare.

"I reconfigured the cameras to show whenever there's any activity in the spectrum that you saw Billy talking to his friend."

I flinched when she mentioned Billy's name. She seemed to notice but didn't say anything about it.

"So if a ghost floats in front of the camera it'll switch to that spectrum?"

"And send an alert."

"Well, I appreciate that, but I shouldn't be needing that anymore," I said.

"Actually, I've been... "

"Wait," I said holding my hand up to silence her. "Do you smell that?"

She sniffed the air.

"Yes, what is that?"

"It smells like… " I said, jumping up and dashing toward the kitchen.

When I threw open the kitchen door, I found Dolores standing in front of the stove. The smell of the delicious food overwhelmed me and sent my salivary glands into instant drool mode.

Marie almost smacked me with the door as she came through, staring as well.

"Well, hello, you two," Dolores said stirring something in a large pan. "I figured you hadn't had a good home-cooked meal in a while, so I took the liberty."

"Is that… ?" I said.

"Beef Stroganoff with mashed potatoes and asparagus."

It was all I could do not to start panting like a dog.

"Have I told you lately that I love you?" I said.

Dolores smiled.

"Flattery, sir will get you fed," she said. "Why don't you set the table?"

In a flash, I had plates, glasses, and silverware out, then dove into a chair as she carried over the courses one by one.

It was tough but I managed to wait for both ladies to serve themselves before heaping piles of deliciousness onto my plate.

The amazing aromas didn't do the flavors justice. It was hands down the most delicious meal I'd ever eaten. And I've had gourmet meals during my vacations cooked by world-renowned chefs.

For a solid ten minutes, the only sounds around the table were silverware along with mild slurping sounds and the occasional belch. I'll let you figure out who that was.

The ladies both leaned back before I finished my last bite.

"Ahh… " I said. "I feel like my stomach and mouth had a mutual orgasm."

Marie rolled her eyes.

"You just had to make it weird," Dolores said.

"Don't I always?"

"Usually," Marie added.

"It at least sounds like you're getting back to your normal self," Dolores said.

"The one who treats my friends like crap?" I said.

"Enough!" Dolores said loudly, causing the word to echo around the room in a way I'd never heard before.

"You can be a jerk when you want to, but you also care about those close to you," Marie said.

I raised my eyebrows up and down at her.

"Not that way," she said, exasperated.

"The point is you need to let Billy go," Dolores said. "Right now he's upset, but in time he might return."

"Is that a good thing or a bad thing?" I said.

"What do you mean," Marie said.

"I'm guessing you haven't told her about your vision," I said to Dolores.

"No," she said sheepishly. "It didn't come up in our conversations."

"What are you two talking about," Marie said, sounding frustrated.

I stared at Dolores.

"Shall I or would you rather?" I said.

She sighed heavily. "I'd better do it so you don't screw it up."

I held my chest as if wounded by her comment.

"I had a vision of Billy killing our esteemed benefactor here," she said, indicating toward me.

"A vision?" Marie said.

"Dolores is… " I said, struggling to find the right words while looking Dolores in the eye. "Special. She has certain abilities, one of which is being able to predict the death of people around her."

Marie sat silent, staring at me as if digesting what she was hearing.

"And you had one of these visions… " she said to Dolores. "About Billy killing him?" she pointed at me.

Dolores nodded.

"So, if we believe this to be true… " Marie said. "Shouldn't we be worried that he might come back here with a gun?"

"That's not how it happens," I said.

"Happens?" Marie said looking annoyed. "As in, you've already accepted this and are ok with it?"

"I never said I was okay with it, but I know it won't happen that way," I said.

"Then how will it happen?" Marie said.

Dolores and I locked eyes.

"I think that's a detail we're not sure you're ready for," I said.

Marie sat back in her chair and folded her arms across her chest.

"Exactly who is responsible for setting up all the security systems in and around this house?" she said. "You don't think I'm ready to handle whatever threats that might come your way?"

"What if I said it doesn't happen at the house?" I said.

Marie hesitated.

"Then I'd say you're grounded," she said. "If it doesn't happen at the house then keeping you here keeps you safe."

I hadn't really thought about it that way. She had a point, but I couldn't stay hiding in my house for the rest of my life like some eccentric billionaire. I wasn't that rich. Eventually, I would go stir-crazy anyway.

Dolores watched me as if reading my thoughts. I wondered if she was able to do that.

'Mind your own business, old woman,' I thought.

Her affect didn't change. Either she was good at hiding her emotions or she really couldn't read my mind.

"The latter," Dolores said, winking at me.

"Ok, that's terrifying," I said.

She shrugged. "You'll get used to it."

Marie cleared her throat.

"We were talking about keeping this man safe," she said to Dolores.

"Unfortunately, I don't think there's a way," Dolores said. "I've already seen it. It happens."

"You seem alright with that," Marie said to her.

"Of course not," Dolores said. "I'd rather he hang around for at least a few more years. As much of a pain in the butt as he is, he makes things a lot more interesting."

"I'm happy to amuse you," I said clapping my hands together like a mechanical monkey.

Dolores laughed and Marie nearly screamed.

"Will you two take this seriously?" she said. "We're talking about your life!"

"I know," I said. "But everyone is in danger at any given moment. Every day in the world people drop dead for strange reasons or things they didn't even know were coming. Car crashes, brain aneurysms, heart attacks, crushed by a piano, it's a dangerous world. At least I have an idea where and when I'll meet my demise. I'm not happy about it. I'd rather be annoying this old woman when I'm an old man, but it looks like that's not gonna happen. I just have to deal with it the best I can."

Marie glanced from me to Dolores and back again, then she got up and left the room.

"I don't think she likes situations that are out of her control," I said.

"It's because of her past."

"What's in her past?"

She opened her mouth, then closed it.

"You'll have to ask her. It's not really my place to say."

"Everyone has their secrets, huh?"

"Something like that."

"Ok, I get it," I said standing and carrying dishes to the sink. "Are you washing or drying?"

She stood and brought dishes over as well.

"I'll wash," she said. "I don't trust you to get them clean."

I started filling the sink with water as she brought the rest of the dishes over. Then I kissed her on the cheek.

She turned to me and said, "What was that for?"

"Everything."

We smiled and joked as we did the dishes.

***

Trees flew past me in a blur as I ran faster than I ever have. I kept glancing behind me to see my pursuer. So far, I had yet to see anything other than receding trees, but I knew he was there.

My pistol was in my hand. I had tried the tranq gun and taser, but he was too fast. I knew this had turned deadly and my only chance of survival was to kill him.

The moon was up, giving me some light to see by, but it wasn't enough to keep me from tripping on unseen branches and undergrowth. My flashlight was gone, painfully swiped out of my now bloody hand. All I had left for light was a headband light that had surprisingly stayed on through the pursuit.

The forest was quiet. Only the sounds of me tearing through and my heavy breathing were heard. Animals and all nightly noises were strangely silent.

I wished I could hide quietly somewhere and avoid the monster pursuing me. But I knew it had to end. Leaving him to terrorize and kill at will wasn't acceptable. I had to do everything I could to stop him here and now.

Currently, that consisted of running away like a scared rabbit.

I glanced back and saw a flash of razor-sharp claws. Before I could dodge they hit me on the shoulder and I tumbled to the ground. He was on me in a heartbeat, crushing me with his body weight, and tearing at whatever he could find.

My leg exploded in pain as I brought the barrel of the gun up and fired.

The weight disappeared as he flung himself backward and out of my line of sight. I tried to sit up and pointed my gun at empty trees.

Painfully I turned to glance behind me, realizing my mistake a second too late. He tore the gun away, leaving only the thumb behind as his claws had separated my fingers from my hand.

I screamed in pain and shock as I watched the blood flow from my missing digits.

My gun was gone. The only weapons I had left were my tranq gun and Taser. But he had already proven too fast for them. Having no other options, I fumbled for the taser with my left hand, but just as I *got it out the claws swiped once again. This time he took my entire hand.*

Blood sprayed from my arm that now ended at the wrist.

He held my hand, with the taser still in it, and dropped it to the ground while standing over me and staring with a triumphant glare.

I tried to think of something defiant and witty to say, but all my traumatized mind could come up with was, "Billy... "

He lunged at me with impossible speed. His claws aimed at my head...

***

I woke with a start and sat bolt upright in bed. I was soaked in what I hoped was sweat. These nightmares had gotten more intense with each occurrence. Fortunately, they didn't happen every night or I'd be a basket case. It was bad enough that I had agreed with Marie on a self-imposed grounding, but after a month I was starting to go stir-crazy.

Yes, she and Dolores would frequently visit me, though seldom at the same time. I think they made a deal to take turns babysitting me so I wouldn't be alone long enough to decide I needed fresh air or companionship.

Ya gotta love them for their dedication, but I was feeling cooped up, and quite honestly tempted to take one of my vacations if for no other reason than to have some quality time with my two lovely ladies from overseas.

Try as I might to entertain myself by spending money, it didn't quite satisfy the way cryptid hunting did.

Oh, I built another dummy corporation and threw a bunch of money at various charities that seemed like they cared about their cause. But that wasn't really keeping my interest either.

I got so bored that I started taking an active interest in the idiots at the ranger station. Buying them new trucks seemed to make them happy. And it wasn't like I was really losing anything. Marie had a knack for making money. And the more she had to play with, the more she could make.

She had hustled and worked and dealt so much and so well that my net worth was approaching ten figures. But it didn't really mean that much when I was under self-imposed house arrest and couldn't get out to enjoy the toys and other things that came with incredible wealth.

Marie must have sensed my restlessness and came to me one day with a surprise.

"Here," she said handing me a bracelet.

"Does this mean we're going steady?"

She rolled her eyes.

"No, it's an alert bracelet."

"Like if I've fallen and can't get up?"

"Something like that," she said. "It monitors your vital signs. If they get below a certain threshold or if you press the button, it sends a location signal to The Man and your personal doctor."

"Why would I need this in my personal dungeon?"

"I think we both know that eventually, you're going to venture outside," she said. "This is just in case something happens."

"Keep it," I said handing it back to her.

She covered my hands with her own and pushed it back toward me.

"Just wear it," she said, her eyes glistening. "Please."

She turned and walked away, wiping her eyes.

I took the bracelet and set it on my bedstand.

It was almost three months to the day when I finally decided I'd had enough. Marie had been sick and didn't come to visit me, so I took my chance.

Driving to the station and walking in was like a breath of fresh air.

As soon as I walked in, Jeff shot out of the chair like a spring launched him.

"H… how's it going, boss?" he said.

"Relax," I said. "I'm not here to run the show, just wondering what's been happening."

"W… what do you mean?" Jeff said visibly shaken. "We've all been doing our jobs like we're supposed to."

"I'm sure you have," I said in what was trying to be a soothing tone before Jeff had a heart attack right in front of me. I guess being tased will make you a little jumpy. "I'm just curious if anything has been going on in the park. Any strange reports?"

"Nothing we can't handle," Jeff said with a mixture of pride and defiance showing through his fear.

"There's been a few hikers injured by an unidentified creature," Nancy said from behind me.

"Has it been identified?" I said turning toward her.

"Nothing conclusive," she said. "Vague accounts from victims say it's large, bipedal, covered in hair. One called it like a weird bigfoot."

"What have their injuries been?"

"Claw marks mostly. One of them was bitten and was examined for possible rabies."

"Any specific place where these attacks have taken place?"

Nancy led me over to the map table. There were two distinct marks in red on the map that weren't very far apart.

"Here's where the attacks have taken place," she said indicating the red spots.

I pulled out my phone and took pictures of the map.

"Anything else I should know about them?" I said.

Nancy pondered that for a moment.

"Oh, they took place one month apart," she said.

Chills ran down my spine.

"Did it happen to be a full moon when they happened?"

She stepped over to a calendar hanging on the wall, flipped up the page then let it fall.

"Oh my God," she said. "I never thought to check. They both happened on a full moon."

I bolted for the door before she was done talking. My truck sprayed gravel as I floored it heading toward the areas where the attacks happened. They weren't very far from each other, so I had a reasonably small area to search.

Parking my truck at a trailhead that was in between the two sites, I loaded up with my equipment. My backpack had been reloaded with a new parachute and my belt held my three standard weapons. A Taser, a tranq gun, and a .45 automatic, with plenty of extra rounds for each. I ejected the clip and reached into a cabinet in the back of the truck to pull out a clip loaded with special silver-tipped rounds.

I stared at them for a long moment and sighed before loading them into the .45 then grabbed two more clips of silver-tipped rounds and put them in the clip holders on my belt.

My nightmare flooded back into my mind, mixed with Dolores' vision. I tried to swallow the fear. This was the life I'd chosen. This was what I was good at. And if I didn't deal with this threat, someone else would have to.

There was no one else.

It was my responsibility.

I should've let The Man take Billy months ago. But I was in denial and didn't want to see what was right in front of me.

All of my bullheaded, self-reliant, arrogant, nonsense was coming back to bite me. If only I had reached out to those who were right there and willing to help me, maybe it wouldn't have come to this. Perhaps if I had hired a dozen men to go take care of this problem for me, it would've turned out differently.

But in the end, I knew, that's not who I am. I love handling these problems by myself. It's a thrill like no other. And as many times as I've cheated death, eventually I would have to face it.

I was about to die.

That thought made me hesitate as I took a step toward the trail and began my hunt.

The only way to save my life was to kill my friend.

As I started down the trail in the fading light, I turned on the headlight strapped to my forehead. It was all I could do to focus on where I was going as memories of Billy flooded my mind.

His smart-alec remark when I bought the first drone while searching for the Jersey Devil.

The truck he destroyed while driving through an empty field.

The absolute terror in his eyes at the prospect of walking through the dark tunnel under the house.

The hopeless feeling of watching Dell tear into him.

The look of utter betrayal when I captured the Mothman.

And the rage burning in his eyes when his ghost friend was taken away.

I never thought this kid would make it this far. I thought he would quit after the first encounter with a cryptid, but he didn't. He thrived on it nearly as much as I did.

As much of a loner as I am, I liked having Billy around, because I saw some of me in the way he wanted to get out there and hunt.

Truth was, I missed him.

I traveled a mile before my thoughts came back to the hunt ahead of me. Noises had dragged my mind out of the past and into the present.

There was someone else on this trail, I could sense them.

My hand drifted toward the taser on my belt. I didn't want to go lethal in case it was some random hiker blundering around in the dark on a trail that's closed at night.

In the end, I guess I'm still a ranger at heart, for better or worse.

The soft footsteps approached slowly from the other side of a blind turn in the trail.

I waited, my taser aimed where the creature would emerge. It seemed to take forever until I saw a light appear and a red dot show on my chest.

Looking down I saw it was a laser just like the one from my taser. I looked up and shone my light on whoever had their sights on me.

There stood Billy, aiming his taser at me.

We stared at each other, each still aiming at the other in a standoff. And then I made the worst decision of my life. I flicked the safety on and holstered my Taser.

Billy did the same and slowly approached.

Awkward silence reigned for a long moment.

"So… " I said. "How's things been?"

"Good," he said with a shrug.

"I see you put the money to good use," I said eyeing his rig that seemed suspiciously like mine, right down to the tranq gun and .45.

"I learned from the best," he said.

"What are you doing out here?"

"I'm sleepwalking."

I smiled in spite of myself.

"I see your rig isn't the only thing you copied from me."

"You think you invented sarcasm?"

"No, just perfected it."

"There's the stupid."

"Yeah, you just happened to be wandering around out here in the middle of the woods where hikers have gone missing."

"No clue what you're talking about," he said with a smirk.

"Right. So you're a big bad cryptid hunter now?"

He shrugged.

"Trying to be."

"Have you caught any yet?"

He shook his head.

"This is my first hunt."

"Hate to tell you but you won't be catching one this time."

"Why, because God's gift to cryptid hunting is on the case?" he said with a sneer. "Well let me tell you something. I'm as capable as you are. I spent the last couple of months working out and training. I can outrun, outshoot, and outhunt you."

"Really? That's impressive. Good for you taking the time to learn your craft before using your skills."

He stared at me with a side-eye.

"What are you up to?" he said. "Why are you complimenting me?"

"Because I'm proud of you."

Now he was staring me down with a full glare.

"Not buying it. What's the catch?"

"No catch. I'm proud of you, but you're still not getting this cryptid."

"Ok, for the sake of argument, why am I not getting this cryptid?"

"Because it's you."

His face turned from disbelief to confusion.

"What do you mean?"

"Remember when Dell killed you."

"I died in the hospital, but yeah."

"He infected you with werewolf venom."

Billy's eyes went blank.

"What kind of game are you playing?"

"No game. I'm dead serious."

"I'm not a werewolf."

"I'll tell you what, pull out your phone and search for the symptoms and how long it takes to fully turn into a werewolf."

He kept his glare on me for a moment then pulled out his phone.

This is where I made the second biggest mistake of my life. Not tranqing him while he was distracted.

I watched as he read from his phone and his face turned increasingly paler the longer he read.

"Why didn't I know?" he said in a haunted tone.

"Maybe because you didn't want to. Not many people go around trying to prove they're a homicidal, supernatural creature of legend."

"How do you know it was me?"

"I wasn't one hundred percent sure until you showed up on the trail tonight. Both attacks happened a month apart on the night of a full moon. When you left, you were just beginning to show signs of the change."

"Why didn't you tell me then?"

"Because I wasn't sure, and you weren't exactly in a listening mood."

"Whose fault is that?" he said through clenched teeth. "I trusted you and all you did was use me."

"I'm sorry," I said. "I never meant to hurt you."

He paused and looked at me with confusion in his eyes and then began screaming the most inhuman sound I've ever heard. He threw his head back and began convulsing.

I took a step toward him, thinking I could help, and then I saw the most horrible thing… the full moon rising.

I turned and bolted down the trail, hoping by some miracle I could make it to my truck while he was still distracted.

That hope died as he landed on the trail in front of me, fully turned, towering over me and glaring down.

"See," I said. "I told you you were a werewolf."

Rage bled from his eyes as he stared me down taking one slow step at a time toward me, flexing his razor-sharp claws as he did.

"Look over there!" I shouted and pointed to my left while reaching for my gun. It had cleared the holster and was almost up to where I could shoot when he dove to the side and disappeared into the trees.

I did a slow pan around, looking for any sign of him, but the only thing that stared back at me were trees.

I hoped that he had run off, not wanting to chance that the bullets in my gun were silver. But I knew that hope was foolish. There was no way he would just give up.

My fears were confirmed when I heard a soft footstep. I knew he was trying to sneak up on me and instinctively threw myself to the ground an instant before claws slashed through the air where my head had just been.

I rolled and came up shooting. Aiming was something for people who had the luxury of time. That wasn't me.

Bullets ricocheted off the trees beside him as he disappeared into the woods again.

My senses went on high alert as silence once again reigned. Not even the sound of receding footsteps could be heard. It amazed me that something that big could move so quietly.

My heart was pounding in my chest. Adrenaline pumped as my mind told me to get out of there.

Another footstep. I threw myself down again, but this time he anticipated my move. Instead of slashing at my head, he dragged his claws on the ground, tearing into my side and making blood fly as I rolled away firing where he should've been.

But he wasn't there.

I thought about digging into my pack and patching my side up, but quickly realized the futility of it when the monster was still actively hunting me, lying in wait to do even more damage.

Painfully I stood and started running toward the trail. If he was trying to kill me, I would at least make an attempt to survive. Sitting in one place, waiting for the next attack was a sure path to an early grave.

My leg collapsed from under me as claws tore through my tendons. I hadn't even heard him approach that time.

Still, I fired where I thought he was out of reflex.

The slide on my gun locked back. I was out of ammo. I ejected the magazine and struggled to load a fresh one in, releasing the slide just in time to pull the trigger as he charged me again.

The gun went off as he was almost to me, claws outstretched, going for the kill. Instead, the bullet slammed into him, and he yelped, spinning away at the last moment as I continued to fire round after round.

He disappeared again. I watched over the smoking barrel of my gun, waiting for another attack. My side screamed in agony when I tried to sit upright and glance around for where he might've gone, or more importantly, where he would come from next. I knew he was hit, I just didn't know where. Could this nightmare be over?

There was a long pause where I didn't hear anything, and no further attacks occurred.

This should've comforted me, knowing that he had paused. The thought that the bullet might've killed him made my hopes soar but also made me sad. I wondered if I had let The Man take him right away when Dell infected him if something could've been done. If nothing else, the hikers he attacked wouldn't be missing and surely dead. Then there was the little fact that I wouldn't be fighting for my life right now.

The silence was terrible. Every moment was like bamboo shoved under my fingernails. I took the moment to eject the magazine and load my last fresh one. If another attack came, I wanted to be ready to throw as much silver at him as possible.

No footsteps. No attacks.

It had been a few minutes of me laying there, bleeding, with no sign of movement. The forest remained silent as if it was also holding its breath, waiting to see if the monster was dead or just lying in wait.

Finally, I'd had enough. I had to know either way. Despite the agonizing protests of my leg and side, I rose to my feet and immediately fell again. Looking around on the ground I found a broken tree branch that seemed sturdy enough to use as a crutch.

Leaving my pack behind, this time I stayed vertical with the help of my improvised crutch. Using my headlamp that by some miracle was still strapped to my head, I scanned around for a blood trail to follow.

It didn't take long to find it. Wherever I shot him it must've hit something vital. There were large drops of blood leading off into the woods.

My mind was divided as I stared at the bloody trail. One side said, 'Get back to your truck and leave.' The other side said, 'You need to find out for sure if he's dead.'

As usual, I didn't listen to the common sense side of my brain. I wondered why it continued to send me messages that I routinely ignored.

So of course, I set off following the blood trail.

Every step was a new adventure in misery. It didn't take long to realize I should've at least gotten the first aid kit out of my pack and bandaged my wounds. Looking down at my bloody side and leg confirmed my mistake. But now I was on a mission to find out if this monster that used to be my helper and friend was still alive.

The trail continued, taking me further away with every painful step from my pack and the hiking trail that led to my truck.

But I knew I couldn't stop now if I wanted to. It was more than a mission; it was an obsession. Not only to find out if this monstrous threat to all living things was still in operation but to prove Dolores wrong.

Maybe it was pride, thinking that somehow, I could cheat death once again. Maybe it was hubris thinking that somehow the rules that applied to everyone else didn't apply to me. That just because Dolores had predicted my death at Billy's hands and she had never been wrong about a prediction, didn't count because it was me.

These thoughts chased each other around my head as I continued limping after the blood trail.

Then suddenly it stopped. There was a pool of blood about the size of a dinner plate, but nothing beyond it. The trail had simply ended.

I scanned around and raised my gun, but there was nothing but trees. As a last resort, I looked up just in time to see him falling towards me, claws outstretched.

Time slowed as I aimed my gun and squeezed the trigger at the same time his claws penetrated my chest. His full weight landed on me, shoving the claws through to my back.

He stood over me triumphantly as he pulled the claws out of my chest, bringing gore with it that was my vital organs.

I tried to say something, but my lungs couldn't push enough air for me to speak. My head flopped over to the side and the last thing I remember seeing was a flashing light on my wrist.

This was it.

After all my adventures, all the useless risks I'd taken, I was done. There was nothing left but an empty house and a full bank account.

Had my life been so useless? So unfulfilling? In the end, was Billy right? Did I really treat everyone close to me like I didn't care about them?

If only I could say one last goodbye.

But what would I say?

Would it be some stupid sarcastic remark?

Would it be some double entendre?

Or by some miracle would I find the courage to tell those closest to me how I really felt about them?

I guess I'll never know.

Breathing had become painful. Every exhale sent rivulets of blood out of my mouth to the leaf-covered ground.

At least I'll die in the woods.

The light faded from my eyes. The last thing I heard was a terrible racket. Not like I could do anything about it. I don't know if it was real or my imagination, but I could've sworn through it all I heard someone singing.

I felt my heart beating slower.

Thump-thump

Thump-thump

Thump...

Chapter 13

The darkness was complete. I looked around but didn't see anything. It was so dark I wasn't even sure if my eyes were open or not. No dot of light appeared to guide me along my way. Not like I expected to go anywhere but down. It was one of those things I never really dwelled on but in the back of my mind, I knew I wasn't a good enough person to see the pearly gates. My experiences with God usually came when I needed help. I, like so many others, would pray those, 'Please help me out and I'll do whatever you want' prayers. Of course, I never did get an answer. Eventually, I stopped asking, knowing there was no answer or help forthcoming.

But now that I seemed to have some time to think about it, how would I react to someone who only ever called me when they needed something or were in a jam? Would I jump up and do all I could to help them, knowing that in the end once they were out of trouble all they'd do was ignore me again until the next problem came along?

Probably not. I'd probably block their number or just not answer when I saw their name come up on the phone.

Why would God be any different?

Ok, I figured it out. I'm in hell. Sitting here in the dark, stewing over my existential failures for the rest of eternity… yep, I'm definitely in hell.

At least Dante's hell had people to talk to and interact with. Maybe I'm too sarcastic to interact with anyone. Maybe that's part of my punishment, being left alone with no one to antagonize.

It could be worse. Billy could be here, chasing me around for all eternity.

Come to think of it, how do I know what's lurking in this oppressive darkness?

I looked down. Or at least I thought I looked down. There was no difference. I looked up, but nothing.

I tried waving my hand in front of my face but couldn't see anything. There wasn't even a breeze from my hand. I tried to sit down but felt nothing. Reaching down, there was no ground or floor. I could feel the bottoms of my feet, they weren't standing on anything.

At least my side, leg, and chest weren't hurting anymore.

Pinching my arm brought no pain, just nothing.

For someone who's used to chasing danger, floating here in this fishbowl of complete darkness was unnerving.

Was I sitting in some sadistic snow globe on God's mantel for him to watch me and be amused?

Chapter 13.5

The darkness seemed to be getting lighter. I could hear sounds again. It was quiet, except for the steady squeal of the heart monitor. It suddenly stopped its long steady tone and began beeping again.

Who the hell has a heart monitor in the middle of the forest?

I knew someone was there with me, I could hear them breathing.

I heard a door open, and someone stepped into the room, then gasped.

"Oh my God, what have you done?" a woman's voice said.

From somewhere very close to my ear I heard a heavy sigh.

"I brought him back," said a voice I recognized but couldn't quite identify.

Being dead can mess with your memory.

The End?

Thank you for reading my story. I hope you enjoyed it and return for part 2, 'More Misadventures of a Cryptid Hunter'. In the meantime, please consider leaving a review. It doesn't have to be much, just a line or two, and it helps other readers know if they'd enjoy this book or not.

I know I ended this book on a cliffhanger and most of you are probably lighting your torches and sharpening your pitchforks preparing to storm the castle and demand book 2 right now!

To give you a little taste of the next book, (and to keep from being skewered) I've included a small sample. Enjoy.

More Misadventures of a Cryptid Hunter.

Chapter 1

You know how lots of people talk about what they were in a former life? Some are more serious about it than others, but it all adds up to evaluating abilities they didn't think they had. Sometimes it's just those seemingly fluke happenings that make people think about a former life, if such a thing exists.

In my former life, I was a Cryptid Hunter.

I see you rolling your eyes and saying, 'Those things don't exist.'

Well, I'm here to tell you that they do. At least I think I'm here to tell you. You see my former life ended when a werewolf, who used to be my assistant, killed me.

I can hear you saying now, 'If he killed you, then how are you still around to talk about it?'

Honestly, your guess is as good as mine. I just got back myself. Once I wake up, I'm gonna have a lot of questions for whoever is around.

***

I opened my eyes and looked around that dark room. It took a minute to realize I wasn't in a hospital. It looked like a hospital, the bed, the monitors, but there was a second bed and a cabinet of supplies I recognized.

I was in the emergency care room of my home.

I know, most people don't have an emergency care room in their home. Well, maybe you should. If enough of us do it, we can put those corporate shysters in big pharma out of business.

In case you haven't noticed, I'm not much for the medical profession as a whole. Especially when it can easily be proven that a large percentage of them are more interested in profiting from keeping you sick rather than making you well. Don't believe me, just look up how and why Rockefeller *really* started the American Cancer Society.

But I digress.

I tried to raise my head, but pain made me give up on that rather quickly. I leaned my head to the side, looking for anything like a call button.

I found one on the bedrail but lifting my arm to press seemed impossible. I tried to swing myself closer to the button, but it was agony. Every part of my upper body was screaming at me to knock it off and lay still.

I was never one for following orders.

With my arms taking the day off, I swung my head over and aimed for the button with my nose. I rocked side to side, ignoring the pain and trying to hit the button that would get me some answers.

As with everything else in my life lately, I overcompensated. Throwing myself to the side my nose smashed into the button a little too hard. I felt cartilage crunch as my nose impacted the button.

I tried not to scream in pain as I caused myself yet another injury. Sometimes I wonder if I'm not secretly a masochist.

I settled back into the laying position, feeling a river of blood flowing from my nose and wondering ironically if after cheating death yet again, I would now bleed out because of my own impatience.

It didn't take long for the doctor I'd hired to open the door and look in.

"I thought you were asleep," he said walking over to my bed in a lab coat that was white at one point, but now was covered in splotches of red.

"I see you had fun bringing me around," I said as he wiped the blood from my nose and face.

He glanced down at the stained coat.

"Not sure I would really call it fun."

"More fun than I've been having."

He stopped wiping blood and looked at me with the most serious look.

"I'm sure."

"Ok, doc, no more beating around the bush, what happened?"

He sighed heavily.

"What's the last thing you remember?"

"Being attacked. Laying in the forest, helpless and bleeding."

He pulled up a chair and sat beside my bed.

"I'm not sure if you're up to the whole story, but I'll give you the highlights, at least what I know."

I laid there waiting for a long moment as his eyes darted back and forth as if reading some invisible document and deciding what information he was going to pass along.

"I was at the hospital when I got a notification that you needed immediate assistance. Fortunately, I was only doing rounds and not in the middle of an operation, so I drove here as quickly as I could."

"That must've been the red light I saw on my wrist. That alert bracelet Marie gave me."

"A rather ingenious idea, by the way. Anyway, I hadn't been here more than a minute until a helicopter landed on your yard and some very military looking men carried you inside. I directed them to this room and began my evaluation. The leader seemed very worried about the fact that your heart wasn't beating."

"Usually not a good sign that you can go dancing that evening."

He chuckled.

"Well, I'll spare you the gory details, but after working on you for a while, I managed to get your engine kick-started."

I smiled.

"So, Dolores was right," I said more to myself.

"Who's Dolores?"

"A friend. Tell me, doc, did I die?"

"When you came to me you were dead, but I don't know for how long."

"So, I owe you my life."

He hesitated.

"I wouldn't be so dramatic as to say that. I just did what you hired me for."

"Modesty, can't say I can relate, but in any case, thank you."

"You're welcome."

"Did anyone say what happened to Billy?"

He paused.

"I was too busy at the moment to worry about anyone other than you."

"So, nobody knows where he is?" I said trying to sit up and falling back to the bed.

"You need to calm down and rest."

"How can I do that when I don't know if Billy is still out there or not?"

"Why is that so important?"

"Because Billy is the one who attacked me. He's a werewolf."

The doctor's eyes grew wide.

"Did he bite you?"

I stared at him blankly. I hadn't thought about it. Everything happened so fast I didn't have time to tell how I was being injured.

"I'm not sure."

"It's extremely important that you remember."

"You think I don't know that?" I snapped. "Dell infecting Billy is what started this whole thing."

"I don't know what you mean."

"I need to talk to The Man Who Doesn't Exist."

"You want to talk to someone who doesn't exist? That doesn't make any sense."

"Do you know where my phone is?"

He looked at me with a blank expression.

"I think it may be in the closet with your clothes."

"Would you get it for me, please?"

"We still have to figure out if you were bitten."

"And I will, by making a phone call."

He rubbed his face with his hands to clear away the exhaustion.

"I don't know how this makes any sense, but then we are talking about being bit by a werewolf. None of it makes any sense."

He went over to the closet and dug through my clothes, eventually coming back holding my phone.

"It's a little worse for wear."

"You should've seen it after the first werewolf attack," I said turning it on and dialing a number.

He shook his head.

"Is this the way this job is going to be all the time?"

"I certainly hope not."

With extreme effort I was able to move my fingers enough to dial the number and put the phone on speaker before laying it on the bed.

The doctor left the room rubbing his neck as the line rang for the third time.

"Who is this?" The Man answered more aggressively than I thought necessary.

"It's your favorite cryptid hunter, who did you think it was?"

There was a long silence on the other end.

"That's not possible," he said. "I don't know how you got this phone but I'll be tracking you down and taking it from you."

"No, wait, it's me," I said. "Who else would have my phone."

"It can't be… " he said quietly.

"Why not? It's not like I haven't dodged death before?"

Again, the phone was quiet.

"Tell me something only you and I would know."

I thought for a long moment.

"You were right about Billy. I should've let you take him when Dell first bit him instead of standing in your way."

"Oh my God… "

"What's wrong with you? This was just another close call."

"No… it wasn't. When your alert went off, we came right away. As soon as it saw us coming, the creature ran away before we could catch him. You were dead before we got you in the helicopter. My medic tried resuscitating you, but you never came around. We handed you off to the doctor, but I knew you were gone."

"Well… I guess doc did an awesome job patching me up then."

"It wasn't possible. From the time we got you until you were in your urgent care room was over ten minutes. You were dead the entire time."

My thoughts chased each other around in my brain. It was a long time before The Man said, "Are you still there?"

"I… have no idea what to say. It sounds like it may have been one of those M-word things."

"Miracles?"

"Yeah, that."

"Maybe I'll come by tomorrow and see how you're doing."

"That'd be great. Oh, and by the way, the creature that attacked and… well, you know. That was Billy. He's fully turned werewolf."

There was silence for a long moment. I fully expected to hear some version of I told you so. But to his credit, all he said was, "We'll talk tomorrow."

###

Discover other titles by Michael Kelso

Short Horror story collections

Horror Novelette

Middle Grade Horror Book

Mystery/Crime Novels

Domestic Thriller Novels

Young Adult Sports Novel

Made in the USA
Middletown, DE
05 January 2024

47088907R00192